true tales of
lesbian lust

show and tell

edited by
nicole foster

alyson books
NEW YORK

Celebrating Twenty-Five Years

MANUFACTURED IN THE UNITED STATES OF AMERICA.

THIS TRADE PAPERBACK ORIGINAL IS PUBLISHED BY ALYSON BOOKS,
P.O. BOX 1253, OLD CHELSEA STATION, NEW YORK, NEW YORK 10113-1251.
DISTRIBUTION IN THE UNITED KINGDOM BY TURNAROUND PUBLISHER SERVICES LTD.,
UNIT 3, OLYMPIA TRADING ESTATE, COBURG ROAD, WOOD GREEN,
LONDON N22 6TZ ENGLAND.

FIRST EDITION: NOVEMBER 2005

05 06 07 08 09 a 10 9 8 7 6 5 4 3 2 1

ISBN 1-55583-923-1
ISBN-13 978-1-55583-923-9

CREDITS
COVER PHOTOGRAHY BY PLUSH STUDIOS/GETTY IMAGES.
COVER DESIGN BY MATT SAMS.

contents

introduction

I remember the first time I played show-and-tell. I was in kindergarten. Like many of my female classmates, I brought a Barbie doll. Unlike my classmates, however, I ended up "telling" a little too much about myself. Here's what happened.

In class, after proudly showing off my Roller Skate Barbie, complete with snazzy threads and a plastic boom box, I cornered my first crush, Stacy, during playtime. Stacy was Japanese, cute and pigtailed, and she went on to become a high school cheerleader—an incurably straight one at that. So sad! But back to the point. On that fateful day, I sauntered up to Stacy with all the cool a kindergartner could muster, brandishing my little doll and asking to see her show-and-tell toy. Stacy had brought a traditional Japanese doll wearing a blue satin kimono, and I'd admired it from my square on the carpet. "Her name is Michelle," Stacy said as she let me take the doll in my hands.

Well, it turns out Michelle and Barbie were about the same size…so, as my sexy reader might imagine (probably because she did this herself when *she* was a budding dyke), I took the two dolls and started a serious plastic-on-plastic make-out session. "*Mwah! Mwah!*" I shrieked, imitating their kisses as I mashed their faces together. Stacy thought it was hilarious. She laughed so hard she nearly tipped over a stack of art supplies.

If only my teacher had thought it was so funny. Instead, I experienced that rite of passage that most young queers face sooner or later: I got ratted out to my parents for doing something dykey. The amazing thing was, I never felt guilty. I knew I was supposed to—not only from the way my teacher stormed over and grabbed the dolls out of my hands but from my parents' good-natured attempts to act like it wasn't a big deal. They told me I hadn't done anything wrong, but their uneasy voices belied them. They told me they were there if I needed to "talk about something." What could I have possibly needed to talk about? Those plastic kisses had said it all!

It wasn't a sexual experience; I was too young for that. But, years later, I realized it was my first lesbian experience. Instead of shaming me, my parents' and teacher's reactions encouraged me to hold more girl-on-girl make-out sessions with my dolls, though I had the sense to keep the activity private. It felt deliciously naughty. I knew I was doing something that was *supposed* to feel wrong, but it felt wonderfully right.

As I read through the amazing submissions for my latest collection of true-life lesbian erotica, I remembered that feeling. Why? Because these sexy writers felt it too. It's an essential part of the lesbian experience. In "First Kiss," Amie M. Evans hides her budding sexual relationship with her childhood best friend, not knowing *why* she has to hide her love but knowing trouble will come if she doesn't. In "Forbidden," Natalie Granger succumbs to her lust for a friend's lover, musing that their affair *should* feel wrong but doesn't. And in "The Lesson," Stefka is determined not to let herself be seduced by a married woman—until she realizes it just feels *right*.

That's why I decided to call this collection *Show and Tell.* These writers have evoked the same feeling I discovered as a little dyke in kindergarten—namely, the unique feeling of finding pleasure where others find fear. More important, by telling us about their steamy encounters, these writers show us how diverse, sexy, and genuine that pleasure is. Now, that's the kind of show-and-tell I like! In bedrooms and bathhouses, on buses and beaches, these gorgeous, insatiable ladies get it on. Best of all, their stories are all true. This is hot stuff! I invite you to turn the page and play show-and-tell with these beautiful women. You just might learn something unexpected.

—Nicole Foster

in a bar, by the sea

●

kristina wright

There are thirteen million people living in the state of Florida, and most of them live near the coast. The ones who weren't born and bred in the Sunshine State—which is to say most of them—ended up in Florida because they were running away from something. Another life, another person, something bad they could only escape by running. So they run and they run until they run out of space and end up by the ocean, piled up like ants on an anthill, staring out to sea and wishing they could run a little bit farther. Some head for the Florida Keys, that sand-and-scrub chain of islands linked together by asphalt and bridges. Some buy boats and set out across the ocean, whiling away idle days on small islands and trying to forget whatever the hell it was that made them run in the first place.

Of course, I could be a little cynical on the subject. I took off from Michigan and the life I thought I wanted, or at least the life I thought I was supposed to have, and ended up by the ocean like every other disheartened, damaged soul. It's been two years and I still haven't figured out what the hell I want, and I've pretty much given up trying. I'm content being the proprietor of One-Eyed Jack's, the bar where I spent my formative years. The bar's original owner, the real Jack, had been the closest thing I'd ever had to a father. Now I run the bar in his memory, keeping the drunks happy and the troublemakers under control. It ain't easy, but someone has to do it.

I was leaning against the bar, listening to two of the oldtimers bitch and moan about the Dolphins, when the door opened and a little piece of my past sauntered in. Her name was Georgia Lee and she had broken my heart.

"Hey, you," she said softly. I'm not even sure I had really heard her over the noise of the television and the football argument, but I knew her voice was smooth and sweet as honey.

"What the hell are you doing here?" I snarled, swiping at the bar with a grungy rag. Cleanliness might be next to godliness, but in Key West, as long as the beer is cold and the game is on, no one much cares.

Two years ago, I'd stood on the other side of the bar facing Georgia Lee. She'd been the owner of Jack's at the time, because Jack hadn't been able to track me down before he croaked. When I turned up, Georgia Lee had decided the bar should belong to me. I was happy to share the place—and my life—with my honey girl. Then one day I woke up to a note on the kitchen table that said she felt like she was suffocating and needed to get away. That was six months ago. Six long, lousy, lonely months. I wasn't in the mood to throw a homecoming party.

"Don't be like that," she said, standing at the bar and looking at me with pleading brown eyes.

There was a time when those eyes could have melted my panties right off me. Not anymore. She'd left me with the bar and her apartment, so I couldn't hate her, but I'd missed her something fierce. Seeing her again, in Jack's, was like a sucker punch to the gut. I couldn't breathe for the ache.

It took me a minute to realize she'd cut her hair. Her long, golden-brown hair had once hung to her waist, making her look like a schoolgirl. I had spent hours running my fingers through that hair and, when I couldn't stand it any longer, wrapping it around my fist and pulling her close. I'd fucked her with her hair draped across my body like a curtain. Her mane had been my cocoon and now it was gone. I felt myself mourning the loss of her hair the way I'd mourned her loss when I found that note.

"Where did you go?" I asked in spite of myself. I didn't want to care. I couldn't afford to care. Everyone I'd ever loved had left me, or forced me to leave them. I was done with it, done with her.

She shrugged, her thin shoulders looking so fragile I wanted to drag her over the bar and never let her go. Something about Georgia Lee had brought out protective urges I'd never felt before. It bugged the hell out of me.

"I was in Miami for a couple months, then I went up to Jacksonville and stayed with my brother for a little while."

I wanted to ask her if she'd fucked anyone else. I sure as hell hadn't, but she didn't need to know that. I was angry, jealous. And hurt. So goddamned hurt I couldn't stand to look at her. I started stacking clean pilsners behind the bar, avoiding her gaze.

"We need to talk."

I shook my head, concentrating on my task. "I'm working. If you wanted to talk, you should have talked to me six months ago instead of leaving me a fucking note."

"Fine. I'll wait until you get off."

"Go home, Georgia Lee. Everything is just like you left it," I said. I'd intended to close her place up and find my own, but I couldn't stand to let go of that last little bit of her. "I'll sleep at the bar until I can find another place."

"I'm not going anywhere until you talk to me."

3

"You're going to be waiting a long time."

She set her jaw in that way I remembered. "I'll wait."

And wait she did. She ordered a couple beers from Riley, one of my bartenders who came in for the evening rush, and other than a trip to the bathroom she didn't move all night. Riley took off around 1 A.M., and it was 2:30 when I ushered Ed, one of the few old-timers I remembered from my youth, out of the bar. I stood by the door, hand on hip, staring at Georgia Lee.

"The bar's closed," I said, sounding as bitchy and worn-out as I felt.

"Yeah," she said. "Now we can talk."

I was too tired to fight her. I pulled up a bar stool next to her and waited for her to say something. Anything.

"I love you."

It wasn't what I'd been expecting and I rocked back on my stool. "You have a lousy way of showing it."

She smiled, running a hand through her shorn hair. "I cut my hair."

"I noticed."

"I couldn't stand it anymore. Every time I washed it or braided it I thought of your hands."

"That must have sucked, being reminded of me all the time." I wasn't going to make this easy for her.

Tears glistened on her lashes. "It sucked being reminded of you because I missed you so damn much, you bitch." There wasn't any heat in her words.

I wanted to slap her. Instead, I leaned over and kissed her hard, biting and sucking at her lips and tongue until I tasted blood. I wasn't sure if it was hers or mine and I didn't much care.

She braced her hands against my shoulders, and I braced myself for rejection. I didn't know what I had expected. But she surprised me.

"I'm going to fall off this stool if you keep kissing me like that."

I knew that breathy voice like I knew my own name. My honey girl was hot. For me. My heart—and my cunt—throbbed.

"Well I'm not going to stop kissing you." I'd think about what kind of fool mistake I was making later. Much later.

"Good."

She slid off the stool and wiggled in between my spread legs. Her body was warm and familiar, and my hands immediately went to her full, soft breasts. I stroked her nipples with my thumbs, feeling them respond to my touch. She put one hand on the back of my neck and pulled me down to her, kissing me fiercely while she groped my tits. Then I felt her hand at the zipper of my jeans, yanking it down. Her fingers found my clit and stroked me roughly, just the way I liked it.

"God, I missed you," she whispered against my mouth, her fingers stroking me hard and fast. "I'm sorry."

"Shut up and fuck me."

I tugged her T-shirt up and mauled her tits, first with my hands and then, when I couldn't stand it any longer, with my mouth.

I stood up and pulled her close so that we were pressed together, tit to hip. She put one hand in my back pocket to keep me close while she finger-fucked me. I moaned as she rolled my clit between her fingers.

"Damn, honey," I panted. "Yeah, fuck me like that."

She kept stroking my clit, the fabric of my jeans restricting her motions in a way that was frustrating and erotic as hell. I wanted to strip down and let her fuck me properly, but I was too hot, too ready. I needed to get off.

I came on her fingers, clinging to her to keep from slipping to the floor. I rested my head on her shoulder as my orgasm subsided, breathing in her scent while she soothed my fevered cunt with a gentle, teasing finger.

She was wearing one of her short skirts she was so fond of, and I knew without checking she wouldn't be wearing any underwear. I slid my hand up between her thighs and found her bare. And wet. So fucking wet and hot I couldn't stand it.

We crab-walked backward, an awkward stagger that would have been funny if I hadn't been so hungry to have her under me. I spun her around and pushed her back until she was sprawled across one of the tables by the window, her T-shirt hiked up over her tits, her skirt shoved up to her thighs, barely covering her crotch.

She braced herself on her elbows and arched an eyebrow. "You just gonna stand there and look at me?"

"Nope. I'm going to eat you."

I dropped to my knees and pushed her legs apart, smelling her cunt even before I could see her. I lowered my head and kissed her mound gently. She wiggled her ass and reached for me, but I wasn't going to rush this. I licked her slowly, from bottom to top and back again. Sweet. So fucking sweet. I pulled back, staring at her, spread out before me like a feast. For one quick minute I considered getting up and walking away.

"Damn, babe," she whispered. "Don't tease me."

She'd been gone six months, and I had every right to be pissed as hell. But I couldn't refuse her. I buried my tongue in her cunt, coaxing her juices out of her and drawing them up to her swollen clit. I teased that tender bit of flesh, nibbling it gently then pressing the flat of my tongue against it until she moaned and clutched at my head. I sucked her cunt like it was a mango from my grandmother's backyard, juicy and exotic, ripe for the picking. Mine.

She whimpered and wrapped her long legs around my back, holding me close in case I got any ideas about stopping. I slid my hands under her and cupped her ass, pulling her to the edge of the table as I pushed my tongue inside her. I tongue-fucked her like that until her juices were running down my chin. "Fuck. Oh, fuck," she groaned, thrusting her cunt up to my mouth so hard I thought she was going to break my jaw. I dug my fingers into her ass, anchoring her to my mouth as she came, then I sucked her clit between my lips and hung on for the ride.

I lapped gently at her quivering clit until she unwrapped her legs and gave me a gentle push. "Stop. Please. I can't take any more."

I laughed, feeling something unclench and let go. "I've heard that before."

She rose up on her elbows again, staring down at me with languid, half-closed eyes. "Give a girl a ten minute break, at least."

"Good enough. Want a beer?"

"Sure."

I didn't move. Instead, I rested my head on her leg and closed my eyes.

"So, do you like my hair?" she asked, stroking my forehead gently.

"I hate it."

She laughed. "I figured you would. I'll grow it out."

"Don't take off like that again."

Her fingers stilled. "I won't. I promise."

I wasn't sure I believed her. But right then, with the taste of her on my tongue and my head resting on her bare thigh, it didn't seem to matter much. Georgia Lee had come home. Home to the ocean. Home to me.

she's a bullet

●

alison dubois

There are women you meet and forget in an hour. And there are women you meet for an hour but remember all your life. For me, Danica was the latter.

It was the 1980s, a time of expanse, freedom, revolt, and change. I was in my final year of college, thankful to be graduating at last. I say "at last" because during my eleven-plus-year reign of on-again, off-again college years, I had finally stuck with a major long enough to graduate.

In celebration of my graduation, I decided to go to a womyn's bar, something I rarely did, but tonight it felt right. My career was on track, summer was just around the corner, and the grounds had just been cut, leaving that fresh smell of grass wafting in the air as I left campus life behind for one of my final weekends.

I hopped into my pale blue Volvo and stared at the sunset, a blend of gold, red, and orange swirls all melting into an elaborate pool. I cranked up Cyndi Lauper's "She Bop" and took off. The landscape made me feel invincible.

The 927 was Portland's premier hot spot for women wanting to connect. For a while I sat in my car, watching couples and singles do the mating dance and meander through the nightclub doors. Except for the flashing neon sign, the place was rather plain.

Inside, maybe twenty women were milling around the bar; a few couples held on to each other on the dance floor. I made my way to the bar and grabbed the last stool before a big, grungy-looking dyke with greasy hair could plant herself there. Her expression told me that if we'd been outside, she might have busted my head, but her cute, built, redheaded companion kept her entertained. Thank God for lust.

That's when I saw *her.* For a few seconds, I couldn't breathe. If you can picture Joan Jett during the '80s, you have a pretty good idea how Danica looked. She wasn't a big woman stature-wise, but her mussed coal-black hair and almond eyes gave her a wild look that undoubtedly filled every room she entered. Her personality sure packed a punch. She was hot! I felt myself drooling.

Her modus operandi was sexy and sassy. And though she pretended to be tough, I knew better.

For a while I amused myself by watching her circulate through the bar. But in my mind, I'd already decided: I was going home with her that night. Oh, I know it was terribly arrogant of me to be so presumptuous, but if you knew Danica, you'd understand: She totally fed off arrogance.

We'd actually met before, unbeknownst to her, before she'd been swept up into the whole '80s "bigger than life" living, back when she worked as a box cutter at our local paper and pulp plant.

In those days however, I hadn't *really* noticed her. Probably because most of her face was hidden by a hard hat and safety goggles. I had known fellow employees first by their walk, and second by their name. Dress was no marker of personality, because ninety percent of the employees wore the same generic white overalls.

But that night I was on my second mint julep when our eyes met. Of course, I looked away. I didn't want to appear too easy. I had to let her think this was her conquest, not mine.

Her shadow covered me like a blanket, and when she leaned against the bar, the same tough, grungy dyke who had looked like she wanted to kill me gladly moved, her redheaded cutie in tow, just so Danica could sit. What clout! Her perfume was my cannabis, making me more and more fuzzy-headed with each breath.

Slowly, I forced myself to look at her. Immediately, her eyes—haunting and luminous—held me. Her mere presence made it impossible for me to concentrate.

"Hi," Danica said softly, extending a hand. Her alto voice sounded as cool as she looked in her all-leather black jumpsuit. The moment our fingers touched, I gasped. Oh, she liked that. From that moment on, her eyes glowed with mischief. "What's your name, cutie?" she asked.

I pointed to myself, just so she'd give a surly nod. "Ally. And you?" I waited politely for her to say what I already knew.

"Danica Dane. What are you drinking?"

"A mint julep," I said shyly.

"Barkey, two juleps, please," she said, then slapped two $10 bills on the counter. Her manners surprised me; I'd expected her to have a "the world owes me" attitude. Her personable side impressed me.

"So, where are you from, Ally?" She handed me my drink.

I took a sip, letting the alcohol roll down my throat before answering. "North Portland, and you?"

In her eyes, I saw thoughts whirl. My turf was *her* turf. Suddenly, her eyes were sharp diamonds, too piercing for me to look into.

"Do I know you, Ms. North Portland? Where do you work?" Danica asked. But in her voice, I heard it— a pause, a hesitancy, obviously preferred anonymity.

"Yes," I said, slowly facing those eyes. Her brows drew upward. She was trying to place me. "Boise," I said.

She suddenly transformed from Ms. Cool to Girl From the Neighborhood. "Ms. Midnight," she said matter-of-factly, referring to the fact that I was the replacement who started after her shift. Immediately, her eyes reflected the recognition. I chuckled, raising my glass to her. She clinked it with hers. "Of all places…what brings you here?"

Something had changed in that moment, but I felt a relief I rarely experienced. Being able to be honest was a gift. "I expect the same as you."

Her eyes met mine. "Oh yeah?" She raised an eyebrow. "And just what would that be?" *Game, set, match.* My head was spinning. This abrupt shift hadn't been my intent. A sinking feeling settled over me. I was afraid the supremely sensuous scenario I'd envisioned would no longer happen. Feeling the fish had already wiggled free of the hook, I abandoned flirtation for kick-ass bluntness. What did I have to lose?

"Oh, it's a Friday night," I said. "And I'm almost done with school. I guess I was feeling good about myself and just wanted to top off the evening by getting laid by a sexy woman." I shrugged, leaving the words hanging between us. Her serve.

Danica laughed. Not a polite "I understand where you're coming from" chuckle but a full belly laugh that meant, *Got you, sucker!* Her laughter caught the attention of everyone within earshot. Immediately my face grew hot, and my heart raced with embarrassment. I needed to get the hell out of there.

I got up and ran out of the club. Once outside, I was grateful to soak in the clean night air. Each step I took away from the club made me feel stronger and better and more relieved. It had been a mistake to go there at all.

Suddenly someone grabbed me and slammed me against the building's back wall.

Before I could throw a punch, Danica's lips crushed mine in

the hardest, most breathtaking kiss I'd ever experienced. Not to be outdone, I shoved her against the wall too, leaving a trail of kisses across her face, neck, and shoulders.

Quickly I unzipped her leather jacket, totally unprepared for what was to come. Danica, for all her tough-girl facade, was wearing one of the frilliest red and black bustiers I'd ever seen. Her supple breasts stared at me. The contrast of her ivory skin against the night sky and blinking light left me awestruck. She was beyond beautiful; she was absolutely incredible. I could only imagine how the rest of her would look.

As if reading my mind, she started to unhook the bustier. Even though my loins throbbed and my brain screamed to see her, a sliver of common sense prevailed and I stopped her.

"Not here," I told her.

"Where? I want you. Now!"

I wanted to comply so badly, but I didn't relish the idea of offering a pornographic show to anyone. Nor did I want to chance being seen by police, who often made random sweeps of the area. We deserved better.

It was hard to think. I looked around. Where? I couldn't take her home, because I didn't live alone and I knew she didn't either. Where did that leave us?

I spotted my trusty Volvo. Hadn't cars been portals to romance through the decades? With that thought, I took her hand and led her to my car.

We were barely inside before Danica began pulling off her clothes and tugging on mine. For once I was thankful I'd parked at the back of the lot.

Not one to be kept waiting, she suddenly had the passenger seat down as far as it would go. She lay prone, staring up at me. I was in her arms immediately, sharing one sloppy kiss after another with her. Her fingers expertly stroked and caressed my breasts, my ass, and my clit. Danica was a pro and knew exact-ly what she was doing, taking her time until she plunged her long fingers inside me. A groan escaped from my lips as her thumb massaged my pearl of pleasure. I rode her hand all the way to ecstasy, then lay sweaty and panting in her arms. For a while she gently touched my face and hair. Her manner was soothing and pleasing. It would have been so easy to selfishly lap up her attention, but I wanted to know this woman I had fantasized about many times.

Now was my chance—the moment when dreams would meet reality. I planned to savor every second.

Carefully, almost strategically, I planted kisses and caresses along her neck, her shoulders, her beautiful breasts. I sucked her taut nipples. Oh, she liked that! She was my purring kitty now, growling with desire. Impatiently she guided me down, down, down over her smooth, pale skin to her ebony curls.

That's when I noticed it. A tattoo of a broken heart, above a faint scar that stretched from her hairline midway to her navel. I hesitated. Then I pressed my lips over it. Danica gasped, running her fingers through my hair. I kissed the length of the scar. Suddenly her fingers stopped; I wanted to know why but I couldn't ask her.

I raised my head to look at her. Even through the shadows I saw tears streaming down her face. Instinctively, I pulled her to me. Almost immediately she began to sob. I held her tight, trying to comfort this woman who was more and more of an enigma with each passing moment.

"Are you OK?" I whispered, wiping away her tears. She nodded. I pulled some tissues from my glove box and handed them to her.

"I'm sorry…"

"You don't have anything to be sorry for. But if I may ask…what happened?" She turned away. Had I said the wrong thing?

"It was a long time ago. I got shot," she said.

"What? That's horrible. How?"

With some reservation, Danica explained. She was sixteen when it happened. She had just gotten her driver's license and wanted to surprise her mother by filling up the gas tank. She'd pulled into a gas station, went inside to pay, and saw two men holding up the place. The criminals were ready to shoot the attendant but shot Danica instead, simply because she'd startled them.

Danica was quiet then, and so was I. We lay listening to the sounds of nightlife, distant laughter, and conversations. I wanted so much to comfort her, but I felt helpless. It must have been such a tremendous burden for her to carry around such pain. I saw her differently now, and I suddenly felt protective of her.

"I'm so sorry," I said softly. "I don't know what to say, except that I'm glad you're all right."

Her fingers traced my cheek tenderly. "Me too. How else were you going to get laid?" she quipped, catching me off guard. "I believe you have some unfinished business, woman." She confidently lay back down. Her resilience was nothing short of astonishing.

"Why, yes, I do!" I said. I shifted my body closer to hers. She had amazed me once again; just like that, she'd managed to make me smile.

I drew in the muskiness of her juices, her womanhood. She smelled like cloves, with a hint of Interlude perfume. Casually, her legs fell open, inviting me in. I gently opened her lips to reveal a plump, swollen clit that looked like a bullet extending from her lips, begging for me to kiss it. I licked its base and felt her hips move as she shoved her clit harder against my lips. I sucked it briefly and flicked my tongue over the tip.

She jerked, crying out in approval, "Oh, God, yes!"

I took my time playing with her, alternating licks with touches and strokes, knowing she was getting closer to her own moment. Then, just as her breathing became ragged and labored and her body grew tight, I thrust four fingers inside her. Immediately she squealed, then she gasped and released one final shudder.

As she lay still and barely breathing, I licked up every drop of nectar before climbing back into her arms. I thought I'd only closed my eyes for a moment. But suddenly the brightness of sunshine heated my face. I opened my eyes.

Danica was gone. For a minute sadness swept over me. Our time together had been too brief. But then it sunk in—I was still naked! I quickly pulled on my clothes, and in my haste I noticed it. On the dash of my car was a fresh long-stemmed red rose. I picked it up and sniffed its sweet, delicate scent.

Peeking out at the world around me, I prayed no one had witnessed my foolish abandon. I was thankful it was early.

I got out of my car and looked at the lonely building that housed the club. In the daylight it was drab and seemed smaller. Not one car was in the lot, except mine. I stretched and massaged my neck, trying to work out the kinks.

As fate would have it, I never spent another night with Danica, but I still have that rose. It sits on my mantle, in a box. And whenever I take it out, I'm reminded of my mysterious woman and the night that will remain a bittersweet memory. Always.

seven lessons from the women's bathhouse
●
regan mcclure

1. CARPOOLING IS THE BEST WAY TO GET TO THE OUT-OF-TOWN BATHHOUSE.
I'd planned to catch a ride with three friends to the recent women's night at the Warehouse bathhouse in Hamilton. I arrive at our meeting spot on time but quickly realize that carpools are exactly like those horror movies where you Must Not Get Separated.

Me: Where the hell is everyone?

Driver: Relax. We're right on time. Hey, there's Lee now.

Lee (locking up her bicycle): Hey, am I early? I haven't had dinner yet.

Me: We'll drive through something on the highway.

Lee: I can't support the capitalist, multinational, agribusiness industry by eating fast food. I'll just run and get a falafel down the street.

Me: Where down the street? I don't see anything.

Lee: I'm pretty sure it's close by.

Me: If we just all stick together…

Lee (leaving): Hey, the others aren't even here. This will

only take a few minutes.

Me: Stop! Wait!

Sandy (arriving just after Lee is out of sight): Hi, sorry, my bus got in late. Where is everyone?

Me: We're all here. If we just sit in the car, we can leave soon. Get in. I'm going to lock the doors.

Driver: Actually, I could really use some coffee.

Sandy: That sounds great.

Driver: How about the Second Cup on University? It'll just take a few minutes.

Me: No! We have to stay together!

Sandy: Hey, Lee's not even here yet. We'll be right back.

2. JUST FOLLOW THE SIGNS TO DOWNTOWN HAMILTON.

Two hours later, our road trip is under way. At this stage of the journey, try to wait for the right road, the one actually leading to your destination, rather than gamble on shortcuts that promise to defy the time-space continuum and move your destination to a more convenient location.

Sandy: I'm pretty sure if we take this road, it'll take us into downtown Hamilton.

Driver: That road that says "Highway 6 North"?

Sandy: Yup.

Driver: With the sign underneath that says "To Guelph"?

Sandy: Yup, right here. We can stop by Guelph on the way and visit my girlfriend.

Driver: Aren't we going south? To Hamilton?

Sandy: Um, yes. Well, you just turn the other way and it'll take us to Hamilton too.

Me: Isn't this bathhouse on Main Street in Hamilton?

Driver: Yup.

Me: Why don't we take the exit that says "Main Street—Downtown Hamilton" instead?

Sandy: Fine, fine. Be that way.

3. TAKING OVER MEN'S SPACES LETS US LEARN HOW THE OTHER SIDE LIVES.

For this one night, the Warehouse is hosting a women's night. As we're buzzed in, we enter a large common space with a single sofa in the middle of the room. The side rooms are painted matte black with plywood bench seating.

I take a tour of the rooms and baths. I don't know why gay men have a reputation for interior design. Whoever decorates bathhouses has obviously never heard of the phrase "600-thread-count cotton sateen." In this particular bathhouse, they haven't heard of linen at all. The beds are hose-friendly rubber mattresses, no more than twenty inches wide, and of course they are just short enough that we look forward to either banging our heads or our heels on the plywood frame.

The place is so bare I imagine they've hidden the real furniture and pulled out a few things they had stored in the garage. Or maybe the real men's bathhouse is happening upstairs, with faux-finish walls and tasteful seating arrangements, while the lesbians are hosted in the unfinished basement.

Suddenly I'm overcome with nostalgia for my teenage rec-room party days.

4. MAKE GOOD USE OF THE AMENITIES.

We get there early, when the place is still mostly empty. There's a large main room, and a locker room to the side with a few free weights and a bench. Since my gym membership has lapsed, I think I might as well take advantage of the weight room and do some exercises. Sometimes I am too cheap for words.

As I lie down to do a few dumbbell flies, I notice I'm collecting an audience. "Don't be shy," I say with a cheerful wave. "There's plenty of steel for everyone."

No one joins me. I guess they all went to the gym earlier today.

5. IF YOU'RE IN A BATHHOUSE, YOU MIGHT AS WELL GET CLEAN.

I stand in the shower for a good twenty minutes before rotating between the wet and dry sauna. The showers are near the bottom of the stairs, a good place to watch people come and go. I flirt with the women who come in to shower with me.

Lee: We were going to go upstairs for a bit. Are you going to come with us?
Me: Maybe later. I need to take another shower.
Lee: Haven't you had at least ten showers already?
Me: I'm a dirty, dirty girl.

6. HOW TO GET INSTANT SEX APPEAL

In Hamilton, I am transformed into the sexiest thing on earth: someone who's leaving town by morning.

Girl: Do I know you?
Me: No. I don't think we've ever met.
Girl: You're really turning me on.

This must be why Torontonians think small towns are friendly: The locals are so happy to meet someone who isn't their ex-lover's neighbor's therapist's dog sitter. Since I'm from Toronto, I revel in the knowledge that I'm totally anonymous.

Me (to a woman in the showers): So, how's the night going?
Woman: I think my boss just showed up.
Me: Wow. Small town.
Woman: I'm actually from Toronto.
Me: Right. I was wondering why you looked familiar.

Weren't we at a conference together last week?
Woman: Oh, crap.

7. HOT TUBS ARE SEXIER IN THEORY THAN IN PRACTICE.
I finally get up the courage to float over to the sexy couple I've been smiling at all night. Kissing them each in turn, I half-float, half-roll across their bodies. I run my hands down the back of one girl, and turn to pull the other woman closer to me, when I realize I've used up both hands and I'm no longer holding on to the edge of the tub. The water jets push me back, and my face dunks in the water. Only the threat of imminent drowning gives me enough willpower to let go of my happy handfuls and pull myself up for air.

Me (draining the water out of my nose): Would you like to get a room, or perhaps some other form of solid ground?

8. WOMEN NEED MORE THAN ONE NIGHT AT THE BATH-HOUSE.
We shut the door behind us and look at each other breathlessly. They're hot, and I'm overheated, and now we can…

Me: Wait. How much time do we have?

Girl to my left (checking her watch): I think they're closing soon. How much time do you need?

Me: Four days at least. And I can think of a few things I'd like to do twice.

Girl to my right: Why don't we just start and see how far we get?

Me: Wait a minute. Does anyone have gloves? Lube?

Left: I left my supplies in my locker.

Me (sighing): I guess it'll only take about ten minutes to go get some from upstairs, fiddle with my locker, avoid teasing from my friends, and return…

They ignore my dithering and melt onto the tiny bed together. Fortunately, someone has left an open bag of supplies in the room. I delicately touch the gloves to see if they're (ahem) used. Nope. They're fresh. I happily put one on, and I'm finally ready to go. I dive into the pile.

[*Knock*]

Voice from outside: Sorry, guys, we're closing. This is your two-minute warning.

Me: I think it's going to take us twenty minutes just to get untangled.

Voice: Now it's one minute and forty-three seconds.

I won't give up so easily. I've come all the way here and finally made it into a room with two beautiful women. They can drag me out if they want, but I might try licking someone in the process, just to make the evening worthwhile.

We steal another few minutes together. Not enough to really satisfy anyone, but at least I can get chased out now with a smile on my face. When I get upstairs, there are only a few people left.

Bystander: I think your carpool left without you. They went outside a while ago.

Me: It's OK. They'll get a coffee on the way to the parking lot. They could be there until dawn.

fast girl

●

rachel kramer bussel

The club is moderately crowded, befitting an average Monday night, open bar notwithstanding. Tonight, for once in a long while, I'm not interested in the free booze; I have plenty of distraction right in front of me, in the form of a lithe little girl. She's twenty-six but often gets mistaken for twelve, and people frequently tell her she looks like one of the Olsen twins. She does sometimes, but she's a chameleon—channeling a new celebrity at every turn. One minute she's Britney Spears, the next she's Elizabeth Wurtzel, and I'm not the only one who notices. Not a day goes by when someone doesn't stop her, thinking they recognize her.

She looks so sweet and innocent, and she knows it, using her simple charms for devious means. Maybe that's why I didn't know she was hitting on me the other day, even though she dropped numerous hints. I liked that she was bold enough to ask if she could kiss me when I didn't pick up on her hints; it's a rare girl who goes that far out on a limb.

But that was weeks ago, before we'd become totally comfortable pawing each other. Tonight we ignore my friend from out of town in favor of occupying our own corner of the couch, oblivious for the moment to the patrons sitting around us. Well, maybe not entirely oblivious. Before my eyes close as I go to kiss her, I see a suited guy next to me, smoothly checking us out, and I know there are others watching us, but I lean over and pull her small body against mine anyway. She is a wonderful combination of delicate and sinful, innocent and devious. She straddles me unexpectedly, her legs opening over me, that mischievous smile on her face. I'm sure people are watching us now—I would if I saw us across the room.

My skirt is a respectable length, slightly above my knee, my legs covered in thick gray tights. There's nothing improper about it, except when I'm trying to make out with a girl on my lap and stay relatively under the radar. She has no such concerns, writhing nimbly around me in her formfitting red jeans and a light T-shirt. It's like a lap dance, but much more personal. We're surrounded by jaded Manhattanites, but I only have eyes for her. I don't yet know that she will become my girlfriend, that I will fall for her so entirely that I'll stop having eyes for anyone else, but there is still something, even this early, that captivates me, and it's not just the way she squirms all over me. She peers at me intently, trying to decipher my essence as her eyes mull me over, her smile sweet and mischievous, curious and playful. In many ways she is like a young girl—she looks the part, and has an optimism that most adults I know have lost. As I sit on the couch, she straddles me with that daring smile on her face, leaning back over the edge of the couch to show off her flexibility. I smile too, utterly charmed by this nymph who, despite all appearances, is even bolder and more shameless than I am.

I pull her toward me, arranging her long blond hair around us, hoping it makes us somewhat invisible. We can only go so far inside the club, but I don't want to leave, knowing the magic will end if we break the spell too early. She pushes closer to me, and I feel her heat through her clothes. I grab her ass and fondle it as she leans in close to me. Her breath is hot on my ear and I can hear tiny moans escaping her. I squeeze her ass cheeks, occasionally venturing lower, seeing how far I can reach, how much I can get away with. Each moan sends shivers up and down my body, knowing that I can do this to her.

We're in public, as open and viewable as possible, and yet this feels as intimate as anything I've ever done. We don't care about the prying eyes because we're in our own world, communicating on a level so intrinsic and primal we could be naked and not care. She presses closer to me. She bends all the way back again, her hair falling to the floor, her yoga skills on full display as she contorts on top of me. For the first time in my life I wish I had a cock, so that I could press it up against her, a concrete way to show my arousal. I want to taunt her with it right at her cunt. I'll have to make do with other means.

I pull her face toward mine, and we kiss, hot and wet and needy, her tongue diving forward to reach as much of me as she can. I bounce her on my lap and pull her even closer to me. Again, I feel like some macho guy, despite the skirt, hair, and makeup, with my girl on my lap to do with as I please. I don't know that this will be the first of many nights we're told that we're causing too much of a stir, making guys' cocks hard, guys who like to watch our swirl of hair and lips and skin. I don't know what will happen beyond tonight, when she gets home to her girlfriend, and I don't care. Nothing compares to the way she looks sitting on top of me, sweet and slutty. It's a tricky turn-on, figuring out how much I can touch her here, out in the open, how many times my hand can skim her shirt to slyly brush her nipples, how often I can grab the back of her neck and squeeze it, scraping my nails lightly along that delicate skin while her head tilts back at the contact. We bring ourselves to the edge, where it almost doesn't feel worth it to stay, where we need to rip each other's clothes off as soon as possible, but then we return, still on edge but composed.

Here, in a too-cool bar, where everyone is trying to out-hip everyone else, a straight enclave in the city's gayest section, we are too fast for those around us. We're too much—too much girl, too much passion, too unrestrained—even though we're quiet and minding our own business. Maybe they sense that underneath our long hair and public kisses, our roaming hands and blushing faces, is something so powerful that we literally can't break away. We don't care who sees us, because we're not here for them. With her, I don't have to analyze every movement. I simply close my eyes as the DJ swirls Madonna all around us and take her in.

I look at her and feel so many things at once—excitement, lust, power, hope, and maybe a little bit of fear. She's unlike any other girl I've ever met, a beautiful and dangerous mixture of sweetness and daring, pushing every envelope she can find. I like to think I'm bold; I like to think I will do anything, anytime, anywhere, but this girl *really* will, and she wants me. She ducks her head down to my neck, and then lower, peeling down my velvet shirt just enough to reveal the bursting pink of my nipple. I've never done anything like this before. Her hair hides most of her face as her lips find my nipple. She licks and sucks it, light and gentle, teasing.

Maybe it's because I don't have a good poker face, never have and never will, and I can't look nonchalant while this fast girl works her magic on me. Maybe we've just caused too much of a stir, finally worn out our lukewarm welcome. Whatever it is, I hear a knock on the wall and am too embarrassed to look up. "That's inappropriate behavior, girls, and you're going to have to stop," says a deep male voice. I mumble something vaguely apologetic, stand up, and hurriedly grab my bags. She is calm and cool; she keeps talking, hugging me, not at all bothered that we're too fast for this place, too out of control. We walk out into the night and laugh, her hand on my cheek as she casts me a look I don't know how to interpret.

It takes us a while to say goodbye, even though the air is chilly and it's getting late. I'm not sad to go, just wistful as she smiles that mischievous smile, promising me even more trouble the next time we meet. She bundles her long coat around her and skips off into the night. *My fast girl*, I think, as I walk to my train, a smile on my face all the way home.

the shortest skirt

●

tanya turner

I've asked her to wear her shortest skirt to the concert tonight and I'm pleased that she has done so—I'm going to punish her later anyway, but I'll have to find a creative "reason" for it. She has an arsenal of short skirts in her closet, ones that rise up the backs of her legs, showing off those delicate thighs, teasing anyone watching with the promise of what's underneath. You can tell that she's the kind of girl who loves to get spanked by the way she wears those skirts, prancing about like she doesn't know her ass is clearly visible. Simply by wearing her skirts she beckons me, and this particular skirt, with its schoolgirl plaid puffing out slightly at the ends, is perfect for what I have in mind.

With this skirt, I can easily let my hands wander, and I do, running my palm over her stocking-covered ass for pretty much anyone to see, squeezing her perfectly round cheeks, hard, so she knows that even though she's worn the skirt she's not off the hook yet. Finally, during a break in the band's performance, I lift her up and sweep her downstairs, into the bathroom. Everyone else will just have to wait until I'm done with her, which could take a while. I close and lock the bathroom door, shoving her up against the wall, pressing my entire body against her. We've both been extremely affected by the hours of groping I've subjected her to; I'm surprised by how wet I am and rub myself against her.

Her hands automatically go above her head, without my even having to ask. That's how much she can't wait for me to spank her. She doesn't say a word as I push the skirt down, leaving it to puddle around her ankles, framing her in the naughtiest way possible. She is caught, trapped, and while she could surely escape, she would never want to. I'm very glad she's worn the requested item, because I don't think I could wait another second to get my hands on her ass. I'd have spanked her anyway, but the skirt lets me at her as quickly as possible, without any pesky layers to get in the way of my true treasure. I admire the way the sheer black tights hug every curve before I peel them down so they rest at the top of her thighs. They frame her pale skin perfectly. I hold her shoulder up against the wall, lest she be tempted to sink down, and bring my other hand back to smack her, hard. The first slap is always the best, the most jarring, and I'm rewarded not only with the sharp red mark on her ass but also her intake of breath. I am practically ready to come myself, but I can't think about that right now as I move to the side and give her other cheek an equally firm smack. Should I linger there, cupping her cheek, fondling her hot skin? Or should I make things even hotter? I move closer, so my head is next to hers, and lick her neck before spanking her again. I get lost in the sensation of smacking her, giving her what she's been dreaming of all night, warming her butt until it could be our own personal oven. I get lost in the way she moves to grant me better access, the way my hand quickly reddens her entire buttocks. I move down to the backs of her legs, treating them to whacks that are sure to sting, challenging her to wait it out. I've brought a few toys with me tonight, but there is no time to get them ready; this is too urgent for amenities. She shudders beneath me, silently begging for more, and I'm more than happy to oblige. I sink my teeth into the side of her neck as I keep spanking her, harder and then lighter, teasing.

By this point I don't care who hears us, and while I am loud with my desire when I'm spanked, she revels quietly in the delicious pain being inflicted. Her nails claw at the wall, trying to hold on to it and her sanity as she bites her arm. I feel feral, raw and primitive. I pinch her skin, first the firm flesh of her ass and then the tender soft folds of her inner thighs, wanting more, always more. I can feel the heat from her pussy, the beckoning warmth of her wet pink flesh calling to me, but her pussy will have to wait its turn. I could stare again at her ass, at its beauty, sticking out just a little, flushed and red like her face. I could stare at her all night, but I don't. I go back to spanking her, making her squirm and sigh and strain. I reach as far behind me as I can, bringing my hand crashing down against her thin body, pushing her into the wall. With her face turned against the hard surface, she lets me pound her as much as I want to.

I know we should be going, but I can't resist and dig in my bag for the paddle I've stuffed in there for just such an occasion. It's a bright, shiny red, the perfect color because it gives me something to aim for, and I bring it down against her with a loud smack, watching it reinforce her blushing cheeks. She moans, and I see her face grimace in arousal; when I ask her if she wants me to stop, her eyes fly open. She stares at me before giving a horrified, "No!" So I keep going, loving the loud sound as it reverberates throughout the room. She can take a lot, and I aim to please, giving her everything she desires and more. I pull and pinch her skin, stretch it out, and keep up the whacks, teasing her by stroking her pussy in between smacks, but never fully entering her. I love to see how long she can hold out, how drippingly wet I can make her with each stroke.

Once the paddle has been used to its maximum effect, I return to my trusty hand. Each smack leaves my palm and fingers numb, warm, and smooth with the feel of the blow. I used to talk to her while I spanked her, tell her how much her rosy ass got me excited, how much I wanted to fuck her, how brave she was for taking it all. But now her bottom has put me in a trance, and all I can do is spank it over and over, silently communicating my most precious needs. I tap her ass on her sweet spot, starting to wind down even though we could both do this for hours more. I finish with one huge, final smack, harder than all the others combined, one she certainly isn't expecting. She cries out, a loud "Oh!" of surprise and need. Without even intending to, I shove four fingers inside her pussy. They slide in so easily, I know I could fit many more inside, but since we've overstayed our bathroom welcome, I slam into her rough and hard, leaning my weight against her as I pin her to the wall. I shove my knee up against my hand, forcing myself deeper inside her, and in moments I feel her collapse, her pussy tightening and unleashing her tender juices onto my probing fingers. I pull them out, and she whimpers, empty, and I shove those same fingers into her mouth. I watch her eyes as her tongue lingers at the edges of my fingers, sucking like a baby. Her eyes are wet, searching. I stare right back, telling her everything she needs to know. I pull up her stockings and her skirt, knowing nothing she could have worn would have kept me from ravishing her like this.

We're not done—far from it—but we do have to exit the bathroom. I could do this all night without tiring. Lucky for us, the night is still young.

forbidden

●

natalie granger

Everything about this encounter should feel wrong, and I guess it does. Or, if not wrong, it's slightly unsettling. If a woman told me she was messing around with her best friend's girlfriend, I'm sure I'd be horrified. But desire is messy. It obeys no rules. So, what should feel wrong often feels incredibly right, especially during an elaborate summer vacation, where all the usual bets are off and anything goes. I treat my night out with Dana as simply that—a fun night out, even though we both know there's more simmering below the surface. After I put on my new hot pink sundress, so light it feels like I'm hardly wearing anything, I braid my hair into pigtails, a perfectly innocent pairing that belies the twinge of arousal I feel when I look in the mirror, knowing I care for reasons beyond vanity. A dash of gooey lip gloss, the kind that can draw all eyes to my lips, and I'm ready.

I get a ride from a friend and meet her in the garden of a women's bar I've never been to before: full of lawn chairs, fruity frozen drinks, and tanned, petite women. In L.A., it's hard to tell the dykes from the straight women; everyone bears a studied kind of casual sportiness, and dressing up is only one step up the fashion rung from dressing down. But Dana has clearly dressed up, in pin-striped pants and a dashing white sleeveless button-down shirt, so crisp and clean, a perfect contrast to my fiery ensemble. Her smile lights up the entire bar, and when she hugs me I wonder if she can feel my hard nipples pressing against her. It's evening, but the sun is still out, looking practically permanent, creating a make-believe urban playground. I check Dana out as I would any other dashingly debonair babe, and I like what I see. I close my eyes and try to pretend that we have just met, that we are strangers in a bar, and it half works. It's only when I step away from what I'm feeling, when she becomes "Courtney's lover" that the situation seems off. But I don't let such thoughts preoccupy me, although maybe I should. Instead, I let the hot California sun soothe me, sink into my skin and bones, and meld me like the best masseuse until I am nothing but mush, putty for her hands. My brain, with all its lingering doubts, gets pushed aside in favor of my pussy's urgent, throbbing heat. We talk about this and that, the words simply a pretext to drown out my fast-beating heart, and we both know it. Every few minutes, her eyes quickly scan my body and leave their imprint everywhere, x-raying my soul when they pass over my lower body. She knows exactly what she's doing, and so do I. Every minute we hold off is simply another minute of protracted foreplay. She offers me a tour of the area, and figuring I may as well see some local sights, not to mention her ass as it moves so smoothly beneath her perfectly patterned pants, I let her take my hand. We both know things are about to get dangerous, but we pretend otherwise, walking breezily along the wide sidewalk, past all manner of brightly clad queers.

We are out on the town in West Hollywood, but it seems like nothing more than a pale imitation Chelsea, which I usually reject in favor of the divier Lower East Side. Is there anything divey in this land of sun and sin? If so, I haven't found it yet. Everything is perfectly polished and presentable, and it makes me want to rip my dress, apply some elaborate eye makeup, tease my hair, and shock these staid partygoers. But I don't. I set my sights back home, giving up on the tension that rests between our fingers on the bar, so close that the tiniest movement would brush mine against hers. I resign myself to a vacation that's perfect in almost every way, and simply give myself the orgasms I crave rather than waiting for someone else to do it.

I ask her to take me home, and like a proper butch, she agrees, with no sign of disappointment on her face. We settle into the car, I give her directions, and as she is about to turn the key in the ignition, I reach over to brush a piece of lint off her cheek. As I do so, Dana sniffs the side of my neck, eager for a whiff of my mango-peach perfume, then plunges her face further into my delicate skin, kissing me. As soon as I feel her nose brushing against me, I know I won't, I can't, say no. Our first kiss unleashes all kinds of pent-up feelings, emotions and attractions previously restrained by social custom. Now, far from home, we have no shame, on a West Hollywood side street where pretty boys walk home from the bars, honking their horns to get to the next party. Without drinks or noise or lights or anything except each other, we have our own party. Suddenly my seat is down, and she's on top of me, and some-how, we fit, crammed into a tiny car, our bodies jammed together as our hands fumble for forbidden skin. She lets me do whatever I want, all courtly customs and roles gone, and I quickly push up her top and sink my mouth around a nipple on a small, perfect breast. I forget she is truly forbidden fruit and lose myself in the smell of her skin: soapy and tangy and salty. She smells clean and pure, and her nipples are so sensi-tive my tongue cannot leave them for a second. I suckle each one, tasting and teasing, while my hands fumble down the back of her pants, cupping her ass.

I feel weirder about having sex in a car than I do about having sex with my best friend's girlfriend. Though I grew up in the suburbs, I was never one for cars and rarely made out in them as a teenager. I thought the fogged up windows were mostly a myth, a convenient cliché used in the movies to avoid showing the action. But after only ten minutes of making out, stripping off our clothes and feeling the heat rise between us, I look up and realize the windows really *are* steamed up. They've become dense with whiteness, like your breath on a cold day. It's a delicious, marvelous realization, and I smile, throwing myself into fucking her with as much teenage abandon as I can muster, needing to make up for lost time, getting it on in cars. She can never be too close; our hands grasp for any bit of skin we can find.

I feel like the world has stopped and it's just the two of us, steaming up this car, making it our own, giving the passersby something to talk about. She slides over me, and my hand bends, pushing my fingers into Dana's wet, warm pussy. I have no idea why I ever resisted this. I close my eyes and let Dana push her way under my short skirt, push aside my soaked panties, and press into me. I do the same, and my hand greedily enters her pussy, and I forget the car's confines as I reach for my reward, biting her neck as my fingers push deeper and deeper into her wetness. She snarls and bites me, and we tussle, as much as we can in the cramped space. I have no time to wish for more room, or for toys, or for anything; I simply try not to explode. Tears spring into my eyes as everything becomes hot.

Within minutes, Dana has figured out how to touch me, her fingers contorting in some way that makes my pussy simply gush. She keeps going, twisting and flicking and bending, stretching me in ways I can't even understand. She lowers the seat to a horizontal position and lies on top of me, her weight pinning me down as I hold on to her neck for dear life. I press my fingers forward and hear her moan as I stroke her, all of her weight bearing down on my hand, as I long to go even further. But of course we cannot get totally naked in such a public place. It doesn't stop us from coming—me soaking the seat as she does another magic trick with her fingers, Dana digging her nails into my shoulder blade as her pussy tightens around me. She shoves her wet fingers into my mouth, making me taste my juices, then runs her digits along my cheek and neck, staring into my eyes as though she will never let this moment end. We finally break apart, and as we make our way to the beach, along shaded, breezy streets, the difference from New York's fast pace is incredible. This is a dream, a cloud, a fantasy, and I let myself believe it fully, needing it to be real.

The car pulls into the beach house driveway, and we pick up where we left off as we stumble into the house. I have a flash of conscience, a moment of pause, but the beach is filled with partygoers who pay no attention to two girls practically fucking their way up the stairs. I find salvation in her arms, soothing the hurt caused by all who have come before, taking my heart only to twist and slam it. Dana rubs me all over, her strong hands making me forget, and I want to do the same for her. I straddle her, savoring the power of having her cunt at my command. My fingers sink so easily inside, I know she could take much more, but I let four in for now. She comes so quickly; I am speechless. When she falls asleep, she looks like a little boy, eyelids fluttering beneath her shorn head. I stay up and watch her, tracing her freckles, savoring the feel of her fingers on my skin.

The sun can make you do terrible things. Anything is possible in that warm, forgiving glare, far from home in a land scattered with temptation. Or maybe it's L.A.—a town built on illusion. Or, maybe it's just my excuse for fucking someone else's girlfriend, like I feel as if I'm part of some bad afterschool special destined to end in fireworks and explosions, anger and smashed bottles. Still, at times it manages to be pure California bliss. I do believe those blazing rays cast a spell, and I'm more than happy to let myself be hypnotized.

Which is how I find myself sunbathing on a deck overlooking the ocean, with a girl I'd never given a second thought to, as volleyball players scurry about right before my Gotham eyes. Never mind the terribly twisted triangle we'll find ourselves in once we get home—our affair is all about the here and now. When things get too heated even for the kinky beach crowd, we go inside, to our waterfront cabana. We straddle each other, straining, figuring out our roles in that first flash of bodily insight. I let go and arch my back as she brings her mouth to my nipples, sucking them lightly at first, and then with more fervor as I let out an approval. She bares her teeth and works magic, biting my nipples over and over, sharp, hard, perfect, until my hard little nubs are flattened, pink and soft and utterly tender. "I bet you can come just from having your nipples played with," she says as she does just that, twirling and pinching them with an expert ease that has my pussy clenching tight. She won't let go, even for a second. I slam my eyes shut, focusing on the sweet, tender pain, opening my mouth with no thought about what will come out. This is the moment I love the most, where the pain verges on pleasure, mixing and melding until I cannot separate the two. They spar like expert fencers—stop, go, more, less—until my body has no idea which is which, knowing only that each begets the other. My body fills with a pulsing energy that feeds on itself, and comes for what seems like hours, I feel magical.

Like I said, the sun can do strange things. It can get you higher than any drug. Throw sex in the mix, and there's no refusing. Everyone is beautiful in the sun's searing glare and all-knowing reach. I would wade into the water for her, run naked along the beach, anything for those greedy, grabby kisses, those strong hands and firm grip, that cunt that always wants more and more and more. As we grapple on the couch, her fingers and mine stroking her pussy with more and more urgency until she collapses in a fierce climax, she shows me why forbidden fruit tastes so sweet. As long as we are under the sun's burning rays, nothing can go wrong, nothing is off-limits, and home is a distant memory.

the postcard

●

moira o'sullivan

I looked it up on a map. We were only six inches apart…on a map, that is. But six inches were enough to keep her out of my reach. The first postcard she sent was from Rome. It was a picture of St. Peter's Basilica and had tiny print on it, rationing out information—its history and strange rituals. In seventh grade, one entire afternoon had been dedicated to learning all about the pope; because they were afraid he was about to die. I remember because there was a similar picture of that cathedral in my book. I remember, because Mrs. Lawson wore her long brown skirt that day, the one with the slit up the side that seemed far more daring when I was twelve than it does now. Funny, the things that stick with you over the years. I flipped the card over and studied her words, her handwriting, the precise way she signed the card, "I'll be right back. Always, Lacey." She said the things I would expect her to, how the holiness of the city made her want to do something horribly irreverent. The same urge she used to get to scream while in the library during study hall. The little cardboard rectangle was the closest I could get to having her in the room with me—a thought that made me shove the card in my back pocket without another look.

The day that she left, she said that she would keep in touch, and as much as I wanted to believe her, I didn't. I knew that she would go off, and pretty soon the adventures of her summer abroad would overtake any thoughts of me that might still linger. Any thoughts of one evening that, sadly, already seemed so far behind us. That was what I convinced myself of, because to believe her and hear nothing for months would have been more than I was capable of handling.

I went with her to the airport and hugged her longer than I should have with her mother standing so nearby. She didn't pull away or stiffen in my arms the way I may have, had roles been reversed. That was one of the things that first drew me to her—how free she was expressing whatever it was she was feeling. It wasn't that she didn't care what other people thought, but just didn't acknowledge that they had a right to think anything in the first place. As I loosened my embrace, she stepped back and took my face in her hands. She looked at me, smiled, and said, "I'll be right back."

We officially met on the bus our school had rented for a theater trip—a treat the senior advanced English class enjoyed each year. I'd known of Lacey for the first three years of high school, but had never had any actual contact with her until that class. She sat at the middle of the bus, which allowed her to talk easily to the more popular kids at the back, as well as the less socially adept, who generally migrated to the front. I sat flanked by two other jocks, grasping enough of their conversation to nod at the appropriate times. My attention, however, was all on her. Lacey Harris, with her perfectly tied plaits and coffee-colored skin. I studied her from my seat, without realizing it at first. It was a problem I'd had most of my life. I would become so intent on something or someone that I would fail to notice that I was staring—forgetting the courteous indifference we were supposed to display toward one another. She was actually in front of me, asking if I was OK, before it registered that I'd been caught.

"I'm sorry, what?" I could feel myself blushing as I spoke, more from suddenly being so close than from actual embarrassment. "Are you OK? You looked kind of funny. And then you looked really pale." She bent over to look me in the eye while she spoke. It was the first time I realized that her eyes were two different colors—one green, one brown.

"Actually, that's just the way I look—funny and pale." I offered a crooked smile and she laughed, just as I'd hoped she would.

It started that simply, and quickly blossomed into something I couldn't label, and didn't much want to. We soon realized that her study period coincided with my lunch, and began meeting on the east lawn of the school to eat and talk and pretend for forty-three glorious minutes that we were simply two women of the world.

Any spare moments we could collect, we spent together. She introduced me to the local music scene, and I taught her how to properly dribble a basketball. Whether it was dancing at an all-ages club or sitting by the river watching the cars crawl over the bridge and into the city, we became fixtures in each other's lives. And so, it was no great shock when time for the prom arrived that we found some way to share that too. We decided that instead of scurrying about in search of dates, we would get all of our single friends together and go as a group. It was far superior to the alternative and kept any of us from feeling lonely.

It was about six o'clock on the night of the prom when I got to Lacey's house. Mrs. Harris opened the door before the chime of the bell had time to fade completely. I stepped inside, wearing my standard sneaks and sweats, with the dress I was fated to wear slung casually over my shoulder.

"Oh, my God! Give that to me, will you?" Mrs. Harris didn't wait for me to obey and hurriedly grabbed the plastic-sheathed dress from my shoulder. "Your mother would have a fit if she knew you were carrying this around like a sack of potatoes! Where is your mother, by the way?"

"She had to work a little late at the hospital. She should be here before it's time to go. I still don't see why you two feel the need to take pictures of stuff like this."

My words chased after her as she brushed the surface of my long black gown repeatedly with her hand and hurried into the next room. She had a way of doing that, Mrs. Harris did— a way of making you keep up with her to keep a conversation going. And so I followed her into the kitchen, where she had clearly spent a good amount of time pressing the sleek lavender dress that Lacey would be wearing—the one that now hung in the corner.

The day she bought it we'd spent three hours trying to find any dress at all that wouldn't make me look and feel awkward, as I was somewhat unaccustomed to dressing formally. My athletic build overpowered each dress I tried, and I'd agreed to try only one more before calling it quits for the day. The purple gown was hanging in the fitting room I'd chosen, having been discarded by a previous shopper. Lacey grabbed it, meaning to put it on the rack outside for garments heading back to the sales floor. A tag hung from its seam: SIZE 6.

"OK, I've tried on like ten of these things and you haven't put on one. That's your size, right? Try it on," she said, adding sarcastically, "Join in my pain, won't you?"

I assumed that she would go into the next curtained area, and a few moments later we would each emerge from our respective rooms, like so many friends in so many movie montages I'd seen over the years.

"Oh, fine, you big baby." Lacey stepped in beside me and began to peel off her layers of clothing. The fitting room was large, more than enough space for the two of us, but it suddenly felt small, and for the first time I felt self-conscious in her company. She pulled off the small green T-shirt bearing her favorite band's logo. Her small breasts stood alert against the machine-cooled air of the room—the plump brown nipples so different from my own bashful pink coloring. I felt the red rush into my cheeks, accompanied by a flash of heat, and turned my face away, hopeful she hadn't noticed.

It was the only dress she tried on, because, just as I'd suspected it would, it fell perfectly over her delicate shoulders and hung from her body like that had been its designer's only intention. I stood there that day and told her it was beautiful, pushing back the strange feelings still pulsing in my chest and limbs.

"Hey, Lace, are you ready for me?" I called as I mounted the steps to the second floor. I wasn't looking forward to having my face painted or my hair pulled into any number of unnatural positions. When she poked her head out of her bedroom door, my breath caught and it took everything in me not to run toward her. Her usually plaited hair fell in long shining curls, tumbling over the ledge of her collarbone. She only asked her mother to use the hot iron on her hair for special occasions. Her eyes were delicately lined with kohl, and her naturally full lips made even fuller with a slick layer of gloss.

"Where have you been? Get in here. I'm nearly done with my face and then I can get started on you."

She skipped across the room to the makeshift vanity she'd created on her desk. She sat down and stared at her reflection, widening her eyes until she looked frightened and sweeping a small black wand over her lashes. I couldn't help but smile at the contrast of her beautifully made-up face and hair to her favorite raggedy tank top and tennis skirt, made of the same material as my sweats. For the second time since we met, she caught me in an undeniable stare.

"What are you smiling at?" It was a second or so until I realized she'd spoken to me.

"Huh? Oh, no. Your hair, it just looks so different. It's nice, just so different."

"Well, you know what? It's your turn now. Park it." Lacey spoke with mock-authority, rose from the chair at her desk, and pointed a stern finger at the seat.

I followed her instruction and placed myself in the chair before her. She stepped back and studied me, brushed the hair out of her eyes, and stepped toward me once more. She took up a small white sponge and some pale liquid makeup she'd had me buy at the drugstore a few days before. Loading the sponge with color, she leaned down and began her work. Suddenly the room shrunk, much like our fitting room had, and I felt the same mix of heat and color traveling to my face. She tapped the sponge lightly under my eyes and then across my forehead. She used a finger to smooth over her work and began to speak softly, needing little volume for how close together we found ourselves.

"You have such perfect skin. You barely even need this. Lucky."

She had just brushed her teeth, most likely right before applying the gloss to her lips. The smell of mint was strong on her breath, and I suddenly wondered about my own. She picked up a small brown pencil from the desk without taking her eyes from me.

"Close your eyes." She came closer and the words brushed against my cheek. I felt a pulse of electricity run through my body, and curled my fingers in defiant little fists at my sides. She slowly lined my eyes. First one, then the other. My nipples grew firm and pressed against the new lace bra I was wearing beneath my hooded sweatshirt. My legs came tightly together, by reflex, not choice.

"OK, look at me," she said as she stepped away to check on the symmetry of her work. Then, as she came toward me to take a second pass, leaning her head closer to mine, my hands reached up and took in the shape of her face, weaved themselves into her hair, and pulled her face to mine.

Her skin was warm, warmer than I would have imagined, as I rubbed her cheek with my own. I moved my lips over hers and my insides gave a small leap as our lips parted in unison and gave way to our eager tongues. My eyes closed. Perhaps somewhere in my mind was that thing that everyone learns about: how losing one sense only strengthens the remaining ones. Maybe if my eyes were closed, I would be able to taste her more fully, feel her more deeply.

Her hands reached up to my face and pushed against me, parting us. She stepped back and for a moment we stared at each other without words, until finally she said, "I'll be right back."

She turned her back and headed toward the door, and I knew that it was over. I had changed everything. It would all be different now. I dropped my head into my hands and wondered why I'd done it in the first place. I heard the door to the room open and then close. I assumed she was running off until she could figure out what to do. It wasn't until I heard the click of the door's lock that I opened my eyes and lifted my head. Lacey checked to be sure that the door was secure and then turned to me. She smiled, blushed only slightly, and then sat at the edge of her bed.

I stood and made my way to her, more aware of my body than I had ever been. There was a tightness in my thighs, a twisting in my belly that wasn't altogether unpleasant. I stood in front of her, uncertain of what was supposed to happen next.

She reached up and unzipped the hooded jacket and slid it from my shoulders. It fell to the floor and made a small clinking noise as the zipper fell upon itself. I could see the shape of her breasts changing beneath her T-shirt. The small, plump nipples I had glimpsed once before becoming hard and pressing against the cotton. She ran one slender finger from my belly button to the edge of my bra, tracing its line to the center of my back, and then running her open hand to the indent of my waist.

I went from being afraid of not knowing what to do, to needing to do something, anything, to be closer to her. I pushed her against the bed and climbed over her, noticing for the first time the dampness between my legs. I kissed her hard on the mouth and felt as her hips pressed against me in response. I returned the pressure. With arms and legs, teeth and tongue, I pressed myself into all of the shallow hollows of her body. I rubbed like an excited animal against her leg, while taking in the taste of her perfumed neck.

She did the same, pulling me, urging me closer, though there was nowhere left for me to go. She slid the strapless, lace bra to my waist and forced me up just enough to allow her mouth at my breasts, devouring one soft pink peak and then the next. I heard my own voice escape in a whimper, a kind of noise I had never made before then. She forced her fingers between my teeth, an attempt to silence me, while continuing to enjoy me in mouthfuls. She turned me onto my back and straddled me. She crossed her arms and grabbed at opposite sides of her shirt's hem and in one swift movement had removed it. She sat above me, the firm of her ass resting on my pelvis, and began to slowly rotate her hips. Tiny circles, she drew tiny circles with her body on mine, increasing the pressure with each new rotation.

Bending over, she teased my lips with a nipple, tracing the shape of my mouth. I took it in, sucking it slowly at first, playing with its taut peak, taking it between my teeth, and flicking it repeatedly with my tongue. She slid her arm between our bodies, and I felt her hand seek out the waistband of my shorts. She pushed against them, moving just enough to get a feel of the panties beneath. The elastic recovered, snapping against my belly and refusing her hand passage. My mouth remained busy, taking in one breast and then the other. My one hand, a fist full of her bed sheets, the other clawing at her back. She didn't give up, her hand more determined in its second attempt than its first, forcing its way past my clothing and finding the well-trimmed hair of my sex.

She brushed her fingers over the soft tufts and tickled the sensitive flesh just beneath. She lifted her body from mine, her one hand remaining in play while the other eased my shorts over the curve of my hips, past the round of my ass, until they reached my knees. Still she hovered over me, blocking herself from moving my clothing any further. And so she swung her body around, until she found herself kneeling over my face. She leaned over, as if lying prostrate before some deity. Her thighs stood at either side of my head like perfectly carved pillars, and above me the swell of her shaved lips pressed against her white cotton panties. I reached up to push the fabric aside, to see the shape of her, the color of her, unfettered. I felt the wetness as I pulled the cloth aside. I stroked her slowly, and then with one finger pressed inside of her. She moaned, a slow hard involuntary moan. And as if to silence herself, she closed her mouth over me, her sound sending vibrations through my body and causing my hips to buck up at her, wanting more. I withdrew my finger and replaced it with two and then three. I moved inside of her, my thumb massaging the small bead of nerves that lie at the summit of her sex. Her tongue plunged deeper with each groan, mine then hers. My arms wrapped around her waist, and I pulled her into me and pushed into her—tongue, fingers, sound, all at once, I pushed into her.

We were two bodies braided into one, as we bucked and heaved with pleasure—crying into one another until finally going limp at each other's sides.

The sound of Mrs. Harris's footsteps warned that she would soon be knocking on the door, trying at its handle and wondering why it was locked. She would hand us the gowns she'd so carefully pressed and would complain for how long we were taking to get ready.

We sat up quickly and put ourselves back together. The knock came and Lacey went to open it for her mother. I grabbed her arm and placed one last kiss on her mouth before letting her go to the door.

Sitting, with the memory of that night still pounding in my body, I pulled the postcard from my back pocket and traced the words with my finger, "I'll be right back."

take it out on me

●

tiffany n. sanders

The phone had rung twice already when Jay blurted out, "Mommy, phone is ringing!"

"Thank you, sweetie," I said. "Go back to sleep." I stared at the phone in my hand, waiting for the caller's number to appear on-screen. Michelle's cell phone number appeared.

"Hello?"

"Hey, baby! What are you up to?"

"Nothing much. Just put the baby to bed. I can't wait to see you." The final words fell unthinkingly from my lips. I hate feeling so vulnerable. I knew she liked to tease me, but she hadn't taken advantage of my "pussy-whipped" state yet. I relaxed into a big smile.

"Ummm, that's what I was calling you about. Chelsea wants to go to the movies and it doesn't start until ten. By the time we get out of the movies, and I take her home, it will be too late to leave her home alone. So I don't think I'm going to make it tonight." She sounded like she had been drinking. Her words were sluggish and I could hear the devilish smile in her voice.

I was silent. I always get quiet when I'm angry. I knew that

Michelle was making excuses, and it made me upset. She was playing me for a fool.

"Hello?" She hated silence.

"Yeah, I'm here. Look, that's fine." I barely avoided saying, *Whatever.*

"Are you upset?"

"No, I'm not upset." I also hated lying, but it was easier than continuing this conversation. "Look, I gotta go. I'll talk to you later. Have fun at the movies."

"Yes, you are upset," she sighed. "It's my daughter, Nicki. We need to spend time with each other. You said you would understand, so why are you upset?"

Why? Because Chelsea is seventeen; you two can go to the movies anytime! Why pick the last movie of the night?! To avoid spending time with me! I'm upset because I haven't seen you all week, and I'm horny as hell! Most of all, I'm angry because I know you're lying to me!

"I'm not upset!" Gotta stick with my fib. "You two have fun. I'll talk to you later." I hung up.

I was pissed. I threw the phone on the couch and went to walk off some steam. Just then, the doorbell rang. *Who the fuck is this?* I thought. *I'm not in the mood for the fucking Mormons, and the goddamn Jehovah's Witnesses have already been by here today. Damn, girl, calm your ass down before you go to that door. God will deny you your own blessings if you keep cursing her/his name.*

I didn't bother to check the peephole or ask who it was. I flung the door open, knowing my body language would discourage any salesman or religious solicitor. And there she was. I was stunned.

"Are you going to let me in?" I stared at her. She wore a Burberry outfit with a matching hat. Beneath its brim, she peered up at me wickedly. She was up to no good, and she knew it.

I stepped aside, letting her in. As I stared at her, time slowed. Her long toes sported a French manicure and gold sandals. Her shaved legs shone. Her walking shorts appeared modest until I saw how perfectly they cupped her ass.

She turned around, inhaled, and stuck out her chest. I felt a huge smile spread across my face. But I gave my complete attention to her erect nipples, which darted the tank top she wore beneath her formfitting open jacket.

"Are you mad?"

Oh, yeah. Thanks for reminding me!

I locked the door and walked past her without saying a word. She giggled behind me. That infuriated me.

I walked into Jay's room to check on him, and as I suspected, he was sound asleep. She slipped in past me and planted a kiss on his little face. He stirred, and she stroked his head until he settled back into slumber.

"Go back to sleep, baby. Misha's here. Mommy's mad at Misha." She smiled and made eye contact with me. I stood my ground. No smile.

I walked away, heading toward my room. Michelle rushed behind me and pushed me forward. I stopped walking to catch my balance, inhaling deeply, but saying nothing. I moved away again, and she pushed me again. She was taunting me.

"You mad? You mad? Huh?" She poked me, egging me on.

So I gave her what she wanted. I turned around, grabbed her hands, and pinned them up against the wall. We breathed heavily, as I felt my pussy juices flow into my panties.

"Take it out on me," she whispered.

At that remark I planted my face into the nape of her neck and started sucking hard. She gasped in ecstasy. I was rough and fast. I moved from her neck to her mouth, ears, and shoulders. Holding her against the wall with one hand, I used the other to fondle her fiercely. Every time she peeled herself off the wall and tried to touch me, I threw her back against the plaster.

I was so fucking wet. Michelle kept fighting me, but I kept her under control. I threw my pelvis into hers, grinding and pumping, over and over. Suddenly I realized we were still fully dressed. My clit was hard. I felt strong, and I knew I could easily rip the clothes from her back, but I also knew better. She would kick my ass; she was a black woman wearing designer clothes. No fabric-tearing here!

I backed off and told her to go to my room. I wanted to punish her for pissing me off. I told her to get undressed and wait for me. I had a surprise.

I hadn't had the chance to tell Michelle that I'd purchased a strap-on. She'd mentioned it in passing once before. I'd told her I had never used one. But I knew Michelle loved it when I took control. And I knew she wanted to be fucked. I went into the spare room, where I had hidden the strap-on, and put it on under my jeans. I walked into the room with a huge boner in my jeans, and Michelle went *wild*. She leapt up to touch it, but I pushed her away. I strutted in front of her, holding my dick like Michael Jackson in a music video.

Michelle bounced up and down on the bed on her knees, like a kid, laughing and playing. Her breasts were amazing. They floated on her body as though they were filled with air.

"Are you going to fuck me, baby? It looks so big. I want to take all of it. Can I see it, baby?"

I loved it when she begged. I stood next to the bed and thrust my pelvis at her. Michelle grabbed the buttons on my jeans and ripped my pants open with one movement. The damned thing burst out of my pants like a snake-in-waiting. She stroked it from head to base, looking at me to gauge my reaction. I was outdone when she put her mouth on it. Damn, that was sexy!

She reached between my legs and threw her head back in delight when she felt my wet pussy. Her fingers went deep and she put her face against my stomach, sucking and licking the dildo as she pulled her hand out of me. She looked me dead in the eyes and slowly tasted my pussy juice from her fingers. It was on now!

I dove on top of her while trying to undress at the same time. I was clumsy on purpose, and she laughed. I kissed her playfully, all over, but the second my lips felt her shaved pussy's moisture and heat the mood got considerably more serious. Playtime was over. It was time to go to work. I laid her flat on her back and got between her legs. Thanks to my newly attached plastic penis I had to roll sideways slightly. Resting my head on one thigh, I lifted the other, bending her knee. I took my time, sucking on her thighs, while using one hand to massage her clit. The other hand massaged her all over, caressing whatever body parts it could reach. She moaned, winced, and squirmed every time I struck a nerve. But I could tell Michelle was holding back. She was afraid to lose control even though it turned her on.

I started licking and sucking her pussy lips. Every so often I dug my tongue inside her. I started with a slow rhythm, then I quickened the pace. Whenever she got to the point when I thought she might come, I backed off and started again with the slow rhythm. It drove Michelle crazy that I could control her orgasms like that. I wanted to push her to multiples, but she always stopped me after one.

When she came, her back arched and her legs clamped over my head. I wasn't ready to stop. I lifted myself on my knees and took her with me—never removing my tongue from her pussy. She was hung upside-down from my shoulders, her body jerking in rapture.

Finally, her body went limp. Michelle panted heavily. She asked to be put down. I complied. Her thick and swollen pussy shone from our combined juices. She closed her legs, and I watched helplessly as my face showed disapproval.

"Come here." I knew she wanted me to hold her. I exhaled

and complied. "Ooh, baby. You are too much for me. I'm worn out and you have just started. I really want to please you, baby, but I don't think I can."

"You do please me! I couldn't be more satisfied. Please don't say things like that, baby. You're scaring me."

"I'm sorry, baby. I just know how active your libido is. If I can't please you, then you will find someone who can." Now Michelle was the vulnerable one.

I turned her around and saw tears welling up in her eyes. She had been hurt before, and was afraid of the same pain again. I understood.

"I'm not him," I said.

I held her gaze until I thought she had soaked in my statement. Then I kissed her softly on the lips. "You are all I need," I whispered to her. She seemed to believe me and snuggled her head in my chest. I folded my arms around her and drew her to me. We both dozed off to sleep.

Michelle's gyrating hips awoke me shortly, though. She was still in my arms, and ready again. With her eyes still closed, she said simply, "Fuck me."

Moving faster now, she grabbed at my strap-on and tried to pull it into her. *What the hell kinda dream did she just have?*

I stopped her and made her look at me. I held her gaze as I directed our bodies into the right position. I sat up and had her straddle me on her knees as I quickly rolled a condom over the dildo. Then I kissed her navel, positioning my hands at her waist. I laid back and said, "Ride it, baby. Let yourself go."

And she did. She came over and over. We fucked for another hour. We fell asleep again, but this time we were too exhausted to snuggle.

I woke up to the sound of Michelle dressing. I was sleeping on my back, and the first thing I saw was the "tent" at my erect groin. When Michelle noticed that I noticed, she burst out laughing. My face flushed with embarrassment, and I rolled to the side to take off the strap-on. She continued to giggle as she jumped into bed behind me, threw her arm around me, and kissed my neck from behind.

"I gotta go, baby. It's getting late."

"I know. Be careful, and call me when you get home."

"Yes, dear," she said sarcastically.

I walked Michelle to the door and waited until she had cleared the driveway. I was already looking forward to the next time I would see her.

if not love…

●

kristina wright

The doorbell rang, and I felt a familiar tingle of expectation. My nipples tightened in anticipation and my response both excited and annoyed me. It was too late to do anything about it, though. Joan had arrived.

"Hello, Tina." She dropped a kiss, neither tender nor passionate, on my upturned lips when I opened the door.

It was almost too easy to imagine myself with her full-time, welcoming home my tired spouse. That image gave way to a more likely one of the bewitching younger girlfriend, desired, yet disposable, when the time came. Girlfriend wasn't right, either, because it suggested an intimacy we didn't have, though I wanted it desperately. I often wondered if that was the very reason she didn't give it to me—because I wanted it so much.

"You look pretty this evening. I like your hair down." Her voice dropped to a murmur as she pulled me close and tangled her fingers in my long red hair. "I can see your breasts through your shirt."

I didn't bother telling her that was why I had chosen it. She already knew. "Thank you, Joan," I murmured, pulling away and reaching for the glass of wine on the table. My hand trembled slightly as I handed her the glass.

I watched her while she drank her wine. She wasn't a beautiful woman, not in the conventional sense. Her face was too angular, harsh even in low light, but she was tall and lithe and had the most amazing hands. Just looking at her long, tapered fingers made me shiver.

Her gaze never left my face as she pressed the glass to my lips. "Drink, Tina."

I drank, and her cool fingertips stroked my throat as I swallowed. She titled the glass too far and the wine trickled from the corner of my mouth. I reached for it, but she quickly caught the drop of crimson wine. She stared through me as she sucked the liquid from her fingertip.

"Come," she said, taking my hand and leading me toward the bedroom. The word was more than a command; it was a prophecy of the evening ahead of us. Standing in front of me in my bedroom, she sighed. "I really love this bed."

The bed had belonged to my mother, and my grandmother before her. It was too big for the cramped room, taking up most of the floor and giving me mere inches of space all the way around. White sheets and a white down comforter offset the ornate brass frame that gleamed in the light of the dozen or so candles I'd lit before she arrived.

Joan pulled me toward the bed, reaching for the buttons of my gauzy blouse. She peeled the cloth away, and I felt like I was shedding my skin.

"I've missed you." I was her graduate assistant and saw her three days a week at the university, but I knew what she meant.

"I missed you too," I breathed against her mouth as her soft, warm lips slid against mine. I caught my breath as she moved down to the hollow of my throat. "I— I love you."

She pressed her fingertips against my lips. "Ssh. On the bed now."

She helped me climb onto the tall bed, and I kneeled in

front of her, wearing only a pair of faded denim shorts. She stood in front of me, stroking the swell of my breasts until my skin dimpled with gooseflesh.

"I love your breasts; they're so responsive," she murmured, taking my nipples between her fingers and tugging.

I moaned low in my throat, my hands coming up to cover hers.

"Hands behind your back," she demanded.

I obeyed, knowing what my cooperation would bring. "Yes, Joan."

The barest hint of a smile came to her lips. "You must have missed me very much to be so agreeable."

I could only nod. In the early months she had compared me to a wild horse in need of breaking. At the time, it had seemed like an insulting cliché, but as I knelt there, my taut nipples between her fingertips and wetness gathering between my thighs, I didn't much care. As long as she didn't stop touching me, I'd let her tame me.

My hips moved imperceptibly, or so I thought, as I rubbed my clit against the seam of my shorts. The relief was bitter-sweet—enough to take the edge off, but not quite enough to give me the release I craved.

"Little slut. Be still." Joan slapped the side of my breast with the palm of her hand.

It didn't hurt, but the sharp sound made me gasp. "Yes, ma'am."

She slid her hand down my belly and over my shorts. I tried not to arch my hips toward her, but I couldn't help myself. She cupped my denim-covered crotch in the palm of her hand and squeezed hard. I moaned.

"You're so hot down here," she murmured, alternately squeezing and releasing. "So hot."

"If you keep that up," I gasped as her middle finger rode the seam of my shorts, "I will come."

"We can't have that, can we?" She took her hand away, and I bit back a groan. "Undress me, Tina."

I blinked, her words barely registering. Then I realized what she had said and reached for the buttons on her blouse. As if in a haze, I fumbled with the buttons until she sighed impatiently and helped me. She slipped off her shoes while I worked on her belt. It was an expensive piece of supple black leather that I had known intimately on other occasions. I shivered.

I unfastened her trousers and pushed the zipper down, my fingers brushing the heavy bulge between her legs. She wanted to fuck me deep tonight. My cunt throbbed at the thought. Her trousers slipped to the ground and she stepped out of them. I reached for the waistband of her white cotton underwear, but she caught my hands.

"Use your mouth on me."

I bent over, still on my knees, and pressed my lips to her cloth-covered cock. She shifted against me as I traced the outline of her strap-on with my tongue. She stood there, hands at her sides, silently observing me. I sucked until the cloth of her underwear was soaked through, wanting to taste her and being forced to taste only fabric and rubber.

"Enough," she ordered, pulling me away by my hair. "Do you want me, Tina?"

I nodded, licking my lips and imagining I could taste her cunt. "Oh, yes," I breathed, my hips swaying in a natural rhythm. "Please, Joan."

"Let me feel you."

I sat up, and her hand went back between my legs. My cunt felt so swollen, almost painfully so, against the tight denim. She squeezed my flesh hard until I made a noise that was somewhere between a moan and a plea.

She pulled her hand away and showed it to me. Her palm glistened. "You're wet through your shorts," she said, sounding pleased. "Taste yourself."

She held her hand to my face, and I licked her palm, tasting my juice. Then I sucked her fingers into my mouth one at a time, teasing her until she pulled away and stripped off her underwear. The cock jutted out at me, thick and pink. She slowly ran her hand up the length of the shaft to the wide head, taunting me the way I'd taunted her.

"This is what you want, isn't it? This is what you need." She smacked it, making it quiver between her legs, a look of sheer pleasure on her face at the sensation it had caused. "Do you want to get fucked?"

I nodded, licking my lips and leaning forward to suck the cock into my mouth, but she stepped back. I whimpered low in my throat. My hips were doing a wicked hula as I rubbed my cunt against the soaked crotch of my shorts. "Please, Joan. I can't take any more."

"I'm going to push you as far as you can go, Tina. And then I'm going to push you some more." She studied me, her lip curling up into something resembling a smile. "Show me what you need, Tina."

I tugged at my shorts, lost my balance, and tumbled side-ways on the bed. I got them down around my knees and plunged my fingers between the dripping lips of my swollen cunt. I moaned, in relief but also in frustration, because I want-ed something—her tongue, her fingers, her cock—inside me.

"Greedy, greedy," Joan taunted me. She grabbed the waist-band of my shorts and jerked them off. Then she wrapped her arm around my waist and flipped me over onto my stomach. "Raise your ass, girl."

I did as she said, my back arched, my bare ass in the air. My fingers never stopped working between my spread thighs.

Her hands spanned my hips and she pulled me back against her. She didn't go into me, not yet. She held me there, quiver-ing against her cock, both of us breathing hard. Then she uttered one word. "Beg."

My mind was reeling with thoughts, but my mouth couldn't form a coherent response. I whimpered, resisting the urge to scream. Finally, in a voice I didn't recognize, I gasped, "Fuck me, Joan. Oh, God, *please* fuck me!"

She thrust into me then, with such force I was driven halfway across the bed. "Yes!"

"Please, please, please," I pleaded, even though she was giving me what I wanted.

She rammed into me, over and over, driving all reason out of my mind. I could feel her emotions in her thrusts, raw with lust and need, as real and as strong as mine. It was only in that moment that I felt like her equal, only when she was fucking me. I was torn between needing to come and wanting to make it last, to feel close to her for as long as possible. Need won out.

I screamed her name as I came, panting raggedly like a woman in labor. She let me come alone, and I knew she was listening to me, watching me, memorizing every detail of my response: the way I gasped when she slid out of my clenching cunt, the way I arched my back and pushed against her to keep the cock inside me, the way I whimpered and trembled like a newborn pup when she shoved it into me again.

When my orgasm had faded to the faintest of ripples, she made several shallow thrusts against me, and I felt her tremble as she came, her breath quickening, her hands tight on my hips. Almost as soon as it had begun, her orgasm was over. She pulled away from my damp body and I collapsed on my stomach. After such a feeling of fullness, I felt bereft at her absence.

She stretched out on the bed, and I rolled toward her, hand still clenched between my damp thighs. I watched the gentle rise and fall of her chest as her breathing evened out. I reached out to lay a hand on her breast, over her heart, but I pulled away.

"Joan, do you love me?"

She glanced at me the way you might glance at another passenger on a bus, as if suddenly realizing you're not alone. "Love,

Tina? I think this bed is getting to you, all romance and frills."

"It's a simple question."

"What do you think this is between us?" She was like that, always answering my questions with questions of her own. It's what made her such a damn good professor. "I know your soul, Tina. I give you what you need, just like you give me what I need."

"Is that love?" I asked, wanting to believe.

"You're pouting." She reached out and tugged at my bottom lip until I felt the slightest twinge of pain. "If this isn't love, what is it?"

A short time later she stood to put on her clothes, frowning at the wrinkles in her blouse. I stared at the ceiling fan as it whirred quietly above me, chilling my sweat-slick body. Once she was dressed, she leaned over and kissed me hard, lingering over my lips until I whimpered low in my throat. Her smile was pure feral satisfaction, territorial and confident. I closed my eyes. I hated that smile.

"Good night, Tina."

I heard the door close behind her and felt the insistent tug of sleep. "If not love, then what?" I whispered in the darkness.

There was no answer.

you can't tell by looking

●

stacy lee

When most people look at my girlfriend Maddie and me, they assume she's the top and I'm the sub. For the most part, I let them, because it's too complicated and not worth my time to explain to strangers the intimate details of our lives. But I'd like to tell you about us, since we're supposed to be sharing a little about who we are. Mad worships the ground I walk on, literally. I know that to look at me, you must think of all the stereotypes about small, submissive, quiet Asian women, but that's not me, never has been, never will be. I'm a bitch on heels, and when I get right up in your face, you'll forget that I'm five-foot-two and you'll be taking a step back. Except Maddie, well, Maddie and I fit together as well as two people can. She may have almost a foot on me, and, being generous, fifty pounds, and skin the complete opposite of mine, all dark, rich, chocolate, but she's as masochistic as they come. All I have to do is sneak up behind her and pinch the back of her neck and her pussy lights up so much I can practically see the sparks. I love nothing more than surprising her, or other people, walking her on a leash at gay pride or having her wear a butt plug that I know is just making her asshole yearn to take my fingers, or my cock, at the end of the day. Maddie is my beloved, my girl, my sweetheart, but also my toy, my plaything. Her size belies what she can offer, what she can give, what she wants me to do to her and for her, as does mine.

Last night was a typical one for us. We both got home from work—I work at a record label doing A&R; she does some corporate high-tech job I don't totally understand, but it's powerful and stressful and comes with an impressive business card and salary—and I lounged in my special, extra-comfy plush purple chair, while she sat on the floor before me and rubbed my feet. She gives especially good foot massages, ones that work as foreplay for both of us. I can always tell when her tenderness gives way to something more, when she's simply aching to take my feet into her mouth, to spread my legs and give my pussy a taste of those perfectly plump lips and eagerly darting tongue. But it's when I know she wants it the most that I always make her wait; that's part of our little game. Today, she holds out, massaging, pressing, working my feet until I'm the one who moans in agony. It feels like her fingers are practically *in* my feet. I look down and notice something missing, and stroke my own neck, pinching right below my chin. She looks up at me, aghast to have forgotten our most sacred ritual. She runs upstairs and back in a flash, and I smile to myself at her docility.

When she returns, she presents the silver pendant to me, the one with half a heart dangling from it. I fasten it around her, watch as she swallows, jiggling the small but tight chain. I have the other half, but am too much of a top to wear it. I keep it safely hidden away, and though I don't often let her see it, it's probably much more precious to me, having her heart, having *her*, than the other way around. I give her a small nod and allow her mouth to travel upward. She nuzzles her way there, over my small calves, kissing the backs of my knees, working her way up my thighs until she is between my legs. I let her nibble her fill on my panties, licking me through them until I absolutely can't stand it anymore and must have the real thing. I hold her head away and peel down the delicate fabric to midthigh, then she settles her chin in the crotch of my panties and licks my pussy reverently.

I always stare at her face, at least at first, and watch the serenity wash over her, like she is finally getting the dessert she's longed for all night. She licks my pussy like it's her last meal, like I'm the best thing she's ever tasted, and I know that I am. Her tongue is soft yet seems to be everywhere at once, darting up against my clit, plunging deep inside, stroking along my slit and teasing me, almost tickling my pussy until I want her to stop, but I force myself to let her keep going, knowing my reward is at hand. I hold open my shaved, bare lips, watch as my clit peeks out, and then finally close my eyes and truly let go. I can feel the little half-heart tapping against me, feel the quickness of her breasts as she immerses herself in my juices, her nose nuzzling my clit as her tongue finds all those secret places I can never get to myself. She takes her time, and these are the few moments when I let go of my dom-ness and let her please me in a way that has nothing to do with power but with giving up power. It's that moment when my entire body relaxes, from the release as my shoulders slump, my eyes close, and my hands go limp, that I can truly come. She can sense it somehow, trained as she is, and revs up her action when she knows my body is most vulnerable. Her tongue darts at my clit, her mouth clamping down around it as she goes after my hard nub, and then she pushes two chubby fingers inside me, instantly finding my secret spot. It's only a few minutes before the combination of her urgent fingers and even more urgent tongue send me reeling, gripping onto the couch, or her head, or simply the air as my body convulses, shivers and shud-ders, tightens and releases, until the final tremor washes over me and Maddie rests her head against my thigh.

After that, it's her turn. She walks up the stairs in front of me, and I grab her ass, pinching the fleshy cheeks, or run my hand between her legs, trying to stall her. She assumes her proper position immediately. Naked, she bends over the bed, her pink pussy lips protruding from beneath her. I run my fingers through their slickness, then tap at her slit, tempted by her wetness, but I make her wait. I cover her eyes with a blindfold, needing her to wait for me, to not see me should I stumble.

I grab the harness, slip it over my slim hips, and add our biggest dildo, bold and black and glittery, one that complements us both. I add some lube, stroke the slickness up and down until the toy once again feels like part of me. I slip into my chunky platforms, putting me at the perfect fucking height, then hold my cock in my hand, positioning the tip right at her moist entrance. This is my favorite moment with Maddie, when I can practically feel our dynamic as if it were tangible, as I simply stand for those vital seconds with the cock head touching her lips but not moving. Of course her inclination is to push back, draw me inside, get what's coming to her. But she never does. She waits, like the good girl she is, the one I saw when we first met as those big, soulful eyes stared down at me, waiting for me to give her permission to kiss me, the good girl she's been to me ever since. Sometimes I wish I could take a picture, the kind I'd thrust in anyone's face when they bring her the check at dinner, or assume she will be the one leading me when we dance. But I really don't care what other people think, and as I finally slide the dick inside her, slapping her dark ass as I do and marveling once again that my small hand can make her flinch like that, it's true. This is what matters: me squeezing Maddie's juicy ass, slamming my cock far, far inside her until she moans, raking my sharp nails along her back while she whimpers, her asking me for permission to come.

I pull out, tease her with that ache, that emptiness, twirl my glittering cock in the air, tap the head against her ass cheeks. I stand to the side for a moment, grateful for my daily efforts at the gym as I spank her, a few solid whacks to each cheek that make her moan in gratitude, then I push her onto the bed, flip her over, and push my cock into her again. Watching her face when she comes is one of my favorite things in the world. Her tongue darts out, her eyes go wild, and she always, without fail, says, "I love you, Stacy," before squinting her eyes shut and letting herself go, her body liquid and yielding as she climaxes. I keep the cock inside her, moving in miniscule motions until she has calmed down. I ease out, pull her close to me, and whisper in her ear, "I love you too, Maddie." Those are the moments that stay between us, and no misguided looks or raised eyebrows can take them away. I'm so grateful we found each other. So next time you see two girls who confuse or confound you, whose size or race or interaction doesn't seem to add up, don't assume you know what goes on with them when they're alone. The truth, one I'm so grateful for, is that you really can't tell by looking, and Maddie and I are proof of that for sure.

fist first

●

rachel kramer bussel

When I agreed to meet with Sarah, I honestly didn't plan on anything more complicated than cooking dinner with her— for me, that's a big enough task. We had mutual friends in common, and had exchanged a few e-mails. When she heard I was going to be in town, she suggested we get together. I was looking forward to a nice, quiet evening; I'd been to a wild sex party the night before and wasn't looking to get laid. I walked in, and a tall, athletic, serious-looking woman in a *Charlie's Angels* T-shirt and shorts greeted me. Like so many people I meet online before seeing in person, she was nothing like what I'd expected.

She'd decided on gazpacho for our meal, and I took over the duties when the onions became too much for her eyes. We ate the cold, spicy soup and talked about writing, politics, and the dyke scene. She seemed pretty conservative to me, and I felt a little out of place. While she was cool and interesting, I got the distinct impression that any thoughts of us getting it on were foolish. Great. Despite the sex party the night before, I'd already started to wonder what she'd be like in bed.

After dinner, I indulged my secret fetish: doing dishes. She stared silently at me while I did them, not talking, and I felt a little uncomfortable. For all my forays into exhibitionism, one-on-one eye contact often makes me nervous. So, when the dishes were done, and she asked me what I wanted to do, I asked her to take me home. That's the polite thing to say on a "nondate"—even if the truth is that you want her to kiss you.

She drove me back to my friend's apartment, stopping the car in the middle of the street and quickly putting on her hazards. I reached over to hug her goodbye, and our faces brushed. I felt her skin and her breath, and I couldn't help it. I leaned into her and started to kiss her. She kissed me back, and soon our tongues sought each other out, sweetly exploratory rather than rough-and-tumble. Which is why what happened next was so shocking. She reached over and grabbed a chunk of my long hair, at its roots, and pulled, hard. I had to stop kissing her as my head fell back, my neck exposed.

She continued to tug, in short, sharp pulls that left me spin-ning and gasping. I started squeaking, making those little gasping sounds that always escape my mouth when I'm on the verge of orgasm. I crinkled my face up, like I might cry, and that's how it felt, like I wanted to cry, or scream—or plunge her fingers into my cunt. I was lost in my hair and her hand, and every time she pulled, I got a little wetter and my pussy ached a bit more. I spread my legs wider in the seat, my plaid skirt rising to the tops of my thighs. She stroked a finger across my throat, and I really felt like I could explode at any moment. I wanted to hike up my skirt and continue, but I couldn't for-get the big streetlight shining down on us.

We returned to her apartment, where I left a mumbled excuse on my friend's machine about why I wouldn't be home. She led me to her bed, and I knelt. I felt like I was shaking, but I think I was pretty still. She petted my head, told me I was a good girl. Again, she pulled my head back by my hair, and I felt a spasm jolt throughout my whole body. It was the most erotic thing anyone had ever done to me, more subtle, yet more direct than any other stimulation. The simple action sent shivers through my entire body. My cunt felt so wet and open, gaping wide, the marionette to the strings of my hair. She drew her index finger over my lips, and I opened my mouth. She slid her finger slowly in and out, and I eagerly sucked it, savoring it like it was her cock. Then things changed. She started fucking me with her finger; I was no longer the active one. She used strong back-and-forth motions. Then it was two fingers, then three, then four. It hurt a little as they hit my throat's far reaches, but I liked it. Whatever part of me she wanted to fill up was fine. I opened as wide as I could for her, wanting as much as she could give.

She moved me onto my hands and knees, on the bed, hovering over me. While one hand continued to work my mouth, the other began to stroke my extremely sensitive pussy. I felt like my cunt was out of control, moving beyond arousal to pure need. It was almost scary. She murmured words that floated over me; only her strict tone resonated. She pulled my thong up so the fabric stroked my pussy and asshole, causing me to arch against the garment, before pushing the wet fabric aside to touch me. She slid two fingers in and out, and I spread my legs for her. I felt more pressure, more tightness. She took her fingers out of my mouth and lay on top of me. I spread my legs as far as I could.

Her body pressed me into the bed. I couldn't move, and I liked it. I loved every move that made me hers, every inch I gave up to offer myself to her. Her fingers became increasingly insistent. And then she stopped—not just fucking me, but moving. Something solid and big and full stretched me out, and I knew it was her fist. Fisting—something I'd seen and heard and read about but had never experienced. But here it was. I was getting fucked in the most intimate way possible. I lay there, taking her, my mouth open, no words. I wanted to cry, not from the pain but from the exquisite novelty. I was her hand in my cunt; my cunt was taking her in. She lightly touched my clit, and I clenched so tightly I got scared I would hurt her hand.

Letting her touch me so deeply, so soon, made me feel vulnerable. I tried to make the most miniscule motions I could, while she found new ways to move inside me, navigating my pussy's most tender spots. I came quietly, almost gently, belying my intense feelings. My last thought before sleeping was one of amazement—not only had she managed to get my cunt to open for her, but I still had all my clothes on. Imagine that.

rock-hard

●

r.b. mundi

Last June I was driving with my girlfriend Charlotte from L.A. to Chicago to see my family during my summer break from UCLA. We decided to take a detour and stop at Joshua Tree National Park. We were both horny and wanted to try something exciting and new. It was the middle of the afternoon, and the desert sun was burning brightly. We parked the car and dashed behind one of the hundreds of huge reddish-brown rock formations that speckle the park like giant confetti.

I pushed Charlotte up against the hot rock and shoved my hand into her jeans. Her pussy was soaking wet, and her panties were drenched with sweat. It must have been a hundred degrees outside; her thighs were sizzling to the touch. "Mmmm," she moaned as I grabbed her cunt and squeezed it like I was making orange juice. "I need this so bad."

I yanked Charlotte's jeans off and tongued the line where her black silk panties met the crease of her thigh. She let out a whopper of a sigh as I teased her, my tongue making tiny circles on her skin. I occasionally lifted her panties with a finger to lick her delicious triangle of flesh.

Charlotte groaned in delight and anticipation when I pulled

her panties to her ankles; she then kicked them off. I placed my hands on either side of her on the molten rock she was leaning against. The heat was like a bolt of electricity that coursed through my body. She grabbed the back of my head and pushed my hungry mouth into her succulent cunt. I wanted her now more than ever as she urged me on with words like "now" and "faster" and "That's it, babe…that's it." I heard a car pass by—and I was certain Charlotte did too—but her sugary cunt was a dessert I'd been craving all day, and I couldn't stop gorging myself.

Charlotte's smooth, pale hips bucked as I curled my tongue around her rock-hard clit. It pulsed quickly, erratically as I enveloped it in my lips, sucking it like it was candy. I readjusted my angle so I could plunge my tongue into her tight hole then fiercely lap at her walls. Charlotte's hands were planted on the back of my head, her long fingers grabbing at my dark sweat-soaked curls. Her pussy was a warm river as I buried my face in her cave, her sharp scent traveling through my nose then taking hold of my body. Shivers darted up my spine and through my shoulders as she moaned and pressed me harder into her voracious snatch.

I heard the roar of another car—no, this time I could swear it was a motorcycle—come closer and closer, then quickly die down. I heard voices too, but they were mere murmurs as Charlotte's heady scent and exquisite taste filled my nose and mouth. I was in seventh heaven; even if someone were nearby, there was no way I would cut my feast short.

"Did you hear that?" Charlotte whispered.

"Yeah, but I'm not about to stop."

Apparently the thrill of being caught took hold of us both, because my own clit was beating hard and fast, and I felt Charlotte's snatch tremble and vibrate faster in my ravenous mouth. I looked up at her for a moment; she was a study in beauty, with the face of a goddess sculpted in marble, burning with desire yet completely in control. When she caught me stealing a glance at her, she licked her lips and said, "I'm almost there. Keep going." But I didn't need any urging as I dove in for her sweet goods, licking her tight button, my tongue diving in and out of her fire-hot hole.

"Let's set up over here," came a woman's scratchy voice. "Can you get the cooler for me?" The voice was so close, the woman—and whoever she was with—must have been right on the other side of the large rock I had Charlotte writhing against.

My own pussy was crying for me to take care of it, so I balanced the weight of my body with one hand against the big rock and quickly undid the button and zipper of my cargo shorts with the other hand. My tongue did cartwheels on Charlotte's clit as I fingered myself, my index and middle fingers hugging either side of my tight, hard knot.

"Do you want this over here?"

"What?" I said.

I looked up at Charlotte, whose eyes were closed tightly. She didn't answer me. The words must have come from whomever had arrived on the motorcycle.

My clit was beating like a drum, faster and faster, in rhythm with my tongue on my lover's sweet spot. Charlotte continued to buck her hips into my mouth; she was close to the edge, and I was right on track with her. My body quaked; fire danced in circles throughout my chest and pelvis. And then I came in a monumental gush.

I knew Charlotte's cunt was about to burst, and I knew she liked it rough and fast, so I flicked and sucked and lapped as quickly and diligently as I ever had.

"Want a beer?" came the voice again.

"Oh, God, yes!" Charlotte screamed, her hips and thighs and stomach melting into me in one incredible rush.

I didn't know how we were going to get out of this one, but I was sure it was going to be good.

birthday spanking, with a twist

●

veronica dillon

Even though it's my birthday, I'm in the mood to give my girl-friend *my* birthday spankings, and she's more than happy to comply. This routine—my smacking her, my taking charge, my planning of just how things will go—feels like a perfect fit, the turning of a lock over and over, until we've hit upon just the right combination. My birthday is but an excuse to fur-ther extend our usual play, drawing it out into an elaborate ritual to savor and cherish, prolonging her punishment in the guise of celebration. I wake up with her tucked against me, curled into my body like an appendage. This will be the best day of my life.

   I never thought that something as simple as the sound my flogger makes whizzing through the air, its purple lashes flying at breakneck speed before crashing down upon her thinly veiled backbone, could be so satisfying, but it is. She quickly awakens, peppers me with kisses and then, with a look of ado-ration, docilely turns over onto her stomach. I see her spine arching up at me, the small, rounded curves of her ass, her flowing blond hair floating around her sides. The same as always, yet somehow more beautiful today, on a new bed, starting a new year. With Madonna's English accent blaring out of the TV, covering the sound of flesh against flogger, I raise my arm and let it hit her, hard, putting every bit of my morning energy into the strokes. I make her count, once for each year of my age, even though we hardly need an excuse, and watch as the suede strands, so simple, soft, and beautiful in slow motion, become something else when hurled with force. They twist and turn, become hard and solid, land with a thud so loud I feel the need to turn the sound up. My family is progressive but not *that* progressive. We don't want to overstay our welcome in their Los Angeles home. The toy feels like an extension of myself, letting me give myself fully to her, holding nothing back as I raise my arm as high as it can go, knowing that for her it will never be too much. Her back is so thin, like the rest of her, that I wonder how she can take it, how it feels as the strands slash against her upper back, yet she moans as each red stripe appears across her backside, then arches up to take even more. I strike and strike and strike, making her count, all giggling gone as we move into another dimension. The birthday is merely a pretense for doing what we love best: transforming ourselves from two giddy, happy girls into a master and her slave.

But still, I feel far removed from any dungeon scene, any false public notions of top and bottom. This is raw, as raw as I am making her skin now as it transforms from pale to pink to red, as it takes, and takes, and takes, way more than twenty-eight lashes. By fifteen, we've both gone off to some other place, removing ourselves from our individual bodies as we meld into one continuous stream of motion. We stop counting once we reach my age, start counting other people's birthdays, and then finally stop pretending to limit what we can do to each other. Today, there are no limits, only magic and trust, sorcery at the hands of a few bits of suede that mean more than a wedding ring ever could. Later, when she fastens the collar I gave her only days before around her neck, always voluntarily (I wouldn't want it any other way), I want to cry at the beauty of it. I've learned that some gifts are better to give than receive, and this is one of them. In turn, I've received the gift of being able to give myself to her. With every swing, every hit, every order, a little part of me enters her. It's a tempered wisdom, not so close to brute force that I can just let myself go. No, topping her requires the most supreme kind of control mixed with a supreme succumbing. I put my entire body and soul into each swing yet never lose my mind. I keep one part of us on Earth, letting the rest fly into orbit as we enter that magical place that helps sustain us through the rest of the daily grind. And when I finally put the flogger aside and rub her back, now so covered in redness I must search for the paleness beneath, the room is charged, heightened with the glow of energy we've created.

We go in the bathroom to finish brushing our teeth and get ready to go out for a special breakfast. Standing in front of the mirror, there it comes again, a wave of desire so huge I know I cannot resist it, despite my growling stomach. She looks so beautifully ordinary, so sweet and sexy as she vigorously brushes, fanatical about her dental care as only someone who professes to loving dentist visits (and job interviews—no wonder she's a masochist) can be. And I have to have her again. Sometimes she is just too much for me, and I wonder if I can go a minute, a moment, without touching her. I will have to later, but right now, I get her all to myself.

"Get down on the tiles." I know she has no idea what will happen next. For a moment, neither do I; I just want to see her on the ground, the way I sometimes just want to see her in the blindfold, or just want something simply because I know she will do it. Because I know I can have it. The mere words spark something between us, solidifying our roles, rendering them innate. She has taught me that actions often speak louder than words, and having a girl willing to do anything I ask is so incredibly sexy and powerful, like being granted my own personal genie. She lies down and closes her eyes, and I push up her short skirt, the one she's just hastily pulled over her bony hips, and touch her pussy through her panties before tearing them away. I know the tile is cold on her ass but that she doesn't care. She is bleeding, but we don't care; in fact, I like it because it will help me get more of myself inside her.

I used to make lists months before my birthday, anxiously awaiting the given day to receive my numerous presents. I'd pore over each one, gleefully anticipating the moment of arrival, until at some point that tapered off and birthdays somehow ceased to matter. Lists and parties felt too showy, too self-congratulatory; who really cared about a single day out of 365 that was only relevant to me, anyway? Gifts became incidental luxuries rather than testaments to another year of life. But she has managed to give me exactly what I want, something I could never put on a list—herself. With her eyes expertly glittering, my hair brushed and gleaming, all ready to go, we lie on the bathroom floor, with eyes only for each other. None of today's planned events, nothing outside this bathroom matters anymore. Now it is only about her hair splayed across the tile, her eyes glassy as she looks at me with awe, lust, and obedience. I press the palm of my hand down on her clit, pressing and pressuring anywhere I think will make a difference, anything that will push her over that precious precipice. My other hand presses against her flat stomach, the one she always thinks is too big and I think is just right.

When she comes, her body silently shuddering, it's a gift that I know exists only in this moment. I don't take it lightly. I want to take full advantage of her, her body, her willingness, this urge to plunder her that I sometimes barely understand myself. But once I am there, once I am inside her, everything makes perfect sense. This feels different than every other time, though I don't have time to analyze it; this isn't something I can compare or contrast; instead it blankets me in a cocoon of want that transports me somewhere wholly unique. "Nobody's ever touched me like this," she blurts, clearly somewhere else, a magical place I have taken her, and I know exactly what she means, because I feel the same way as I push deeper, my hand slippery. I slide inside her, eased by her blood and come and desire. Some say our bodies were not intended for homosexuality, but if that were the case, this wouldn't feel so sacred, or fit so easily. It's as if my hand was always meant to be inside her. She pushes back as I push in—a concerted, messy, glorious effort—and as I fuck her I can't help but think that she is the best and only birthday present I need. Maybe it's a sign of maturity, a gift granted that I hadn't even known I'd wanted: Making someone else happy lifts me higher than any wrapped department store offering or lavish ornamentation ever could.

To be able to take her so high—to push her to new heights while keeping her safe in my arms—is the most special kind of blessing. I've never felt anything quite like this. I want it to make perfect sense; I want there to be a logical explanation for the way my heart races when I push my hand through the bloody doorway to her cunt. I want to know why my pussy twinges, why my eyes fill up, why my whole body flushes with love. Is it because she is so eager to let me do whatever I want, trusting me to give her the pleasure she so clearly wants? Is it because doing so turns out to be so easy, easier with her than any girl I've ever known, like a wind-up toy, where a simple button sets her off? Is it because every time my fingers stroke that beautiful space between her legs I feel like I am seeing the real her, the one that's hidden by her giant-toothed, people-pleasing smiles, the one covered in layers of color and powder, teased with miniskirts and clingy shirts, anything to block others' view? Is it because it's her real self that tightens around my hand as she lets me go where no one has ever gone before, straight into her heart, a direct path that feels like the yellow brick road and the stairway to heaven combined? Now the only one she has to please is herself, and she does, forcing me to give her more and more, until we are nothing but raw muscle and sinew, fierce desire bottled, a brew so potent it could sweep us far away. She is not just giving herself to me but grabbing, demanding, forcing me to fuck her with no trace of anything but pure desire. For tearing me away from my garbled thoughts, for pulling me out of the nightmares that plague me, and for plunging me, literally, into her, I am forever grateful.

I don't have time to stop and think in the moment, but later I am filled with the pride of knowing I have done something I couldn't have done a year ago. She has made me into someone who can give her what she needs and appreciate the awe of her proffered backside, or front, every body part a test and a challenge, a true gift. Some might say it's a selfish one, but I see how much she has to give up to let me hit her, to let me take over, invade her.

I didn't know, at the time, that there wouldn't be other birthdays like that one. I didn't know it was a one-shot deal, but even if I had, I wouldn't have done anything differently. That day is sealed, encapsulated in a perfect bubble, as the best birthdays deserve. Now that things have changed, instead of resorting to tears, I think of that room we consecrated with screams and smacks and blood and love. I think of my hand sliding inside her magic box, finding hidden treasure, her hair strewn across the floor, her eyes so deep and wide and open, like her cunt. I think of rolling over, pinning her down, squeezing that perfect ass as I pondered exactly how to administer that birthday spanking. Most of all, I remember waking up, that first dawning moment of recognition. I reach out, feel around for her still, and there she is, the curve of her ass just as real in memory as it was on that most precious of birthdays, promising not only to be a wonderful day but a wonderful year. That perfect moment is the one I keep in my mind. It will keep me young, inspiring me during times when I have no one to lay across my lap except those who exist in my imagination, beckoning those creatures forth, out of the air, the city, wherever they are hiding, to come take their place amidst the candles and cupcakes of future birthdays. I'm forever humbled by that memory. I am forever wise, humbled, and awed at her ongoing gifts. And I don't need another birthday to remind me.

bare up a tree

●

heather towne

My girlfriend, Emily, and I were browning our hot little bods in the backyard when the guy my Dad had hired to do yard work started mowing the lawn. He was a fine looking stud in his early twenties, which made him almost an old man compared to us eighteen-year-olds, and he showed off his big, sweaty muscles in a tank top and pair of shorts.

"Kinda cute, huh, girl?" I said to Emily, as Mow Man revved his engine at the far end of the yard. He stole quick glances at us as he traversed the lawn.

Emily propped herself up on her elbows, lifted her sunglasses, and smiled wickedly. "Yeah, baby. Mama likes 'im," she said, gently rolling an excited nipple through her bikini top's thin green material. Emily has a lush body, tanned deep brown, with big, heavy boobs that stretch out all her clothes in a most appealing manner. She's got long blonde hair and clear blue eyes—the all-American California girl—and I'm built along similar lines.

She and I generally fool around only with each other, but we aren't averse to some meat in our sexual diet every now and then. I watched Emily's nipple harden. That, plus the sight of the hardworking handyman, got my shaved cunny as slick as the rest of my oiled bod. I rubbed myself through the eensy-weensy yellow bikini I was barely wearing. "What say we give Lawn Boy a scene that will really make him work up a lather?" I suggested.

"You wanna go visit the tree house again, baby?" Emily responded, grinning from ear to ear.

I nodded.

"Sounds like a plan," she said. "You want your hired hand to lend *us* a hand?"

I thought for a moment, then said, "Nah. Not at first, any-way." I jumped up and ran to the giant oak that housed my lit-tle brother's tree fort. Emily and I had fucked our brains out in there several times when my parents had been away. It was twenty feet above ground, so our wicked ways were only visi-ble to spy satellites and horny woodpeckers.

I scampered up the tree trunk's steps with Emily right on my tight little ass, and then, once inside the plywood play-house, we looked down at the poor guy who was chained to the earth and his job. He stared up at us forlornly. We dropped to our knees on the tree house's indoor-outdoor carpeting as Emily gripped my ripe melons, feeling them up while kissing and licking my long neck. Her thick pink tongue traced lines of fire across my sun-heated skin.

I closed my eyes and moaned as her hands pushed my top aside and fondled my naked, tingling titties, plucking and twirling my engorged, rosy nipples with talented fingers. I grabbed the saucy teenager in my arms and pushed her back-ward onto the floor of the skybox. I covered her hot, luscious body with mine, our big, bold boobs pressing together urgent-ly as we Frenched each other.

We tore off the rest of our clothing, tossing the bikinis out the window. And in the blink of an eye, we were in the sixty-nine position—me on the bottom, Emily on top. I gripped my gorgeous girl's taut buns, pulled her puffy lips down to my mouth, teased her clitty with my tongue, and then hard-licked her soaking wet cunny from clit to crack.

"Oh, yeah, Pam," she moaned, her ass jumping in my hands. "Tongue me, baby!"

I lapped and lapped at her cute, bare cunny, savoring her sweet girl juices, and she spread my legs and probed my damp slit with her muff-pleaser. "Yes, Emily," I breathed into her drenched snatch. "That's the way."

My head grew dizzy and my body trembled as she swirled her tongue over my swollen clit, then took it in her mouth and sucked it. She dug two of her purple-tipped fingers into my cunny and started pumping. Her impassioned pussy work, not to mention the intoxicating scent and heavenly taste of her own dripping twat, soon rocketed me to the point of no return. "I'm gonna come!" I screamed for all the world to hear.

She redoubled her already frantic efforts, polishing my buzzer with her tongue while she feverishly finger-fucked me. I buried my face in her smoldering gash, desperate to stave off orgasm, and used my hardened blade of a tongue to fuck her. Her body jerked in my sweaty hands, and she cried out in ecstasy. Hot come flooded my mouth. I gulped her erupting joy, even as I was blistered by my own orgasm. We clung to each other's thrashing, glistening bodies, lapping determinedly at each other's gushing cunnies, and came and came and came in a frenzy of girl love.

Eventually, when we'd calmed down enough to remember that we were still on planet Earth, Emily peeped her come-slick nose out the window and giggled at one of the planet's other occupants. I crawled over to join her. The poor, lonely green thumb with the burning red ears and bulging hard-on was right at the base of our fuck-tree, clutching our bikinis and stroking his shaft.

Emily looked at me and grinned, then kissed me on the lips

and tongued away some of her come. "Wanna invite him up?"

"No way! I'm not sharing!" I yelped, catching the naughty vixen's slippery tongue between my teeth and sucking on it for a moment. I stood up, pulling Emily along with me, and we proceeded to give the horny yard hunk some visual stimulation to go with the aural, Frenching like crazy. We didn't let him climb the tree to paw at its fruit, though.

bewitched

●

amber dane

When I meet Sofia, her hair entrances me. Even in New York, amidst the wildly colored rainbows and seemingly endless array of hair fashions, hers stands out. It's long and flame-colored, gleaming down her back, clearly dyed but still natural looking. I can't tear my eyes from it. The bright, fiery orange, with some lighter streaks of blond on the edges, suits her. Once I see her I can't picture her with hair of any other color. The word *flame* describes the rest of her too—in fact, I think it could be her name as she rattles off all the parties she's been to recently, the photo shoots she's worked, and the concerts she's attended. Her upcoming weekend social calendar leaves me dizzy. Her energy whirls around her blazing head, and I'm smitten.

That night I don't know if she's queer, but I don't care. I'm content to play with her hair and let her make of it what she will. I reach across the tables and touch it, looking up at her in wonder. For all the chemicals it must contain, it's unimaginably soft. I keep stroking it, staring into her face. She's so full of life, such a refreshing change of pace from the usual morose aloofness of city girls and boys. She tells me about a special oil she uses on her hair, which she calls witch's oil, and I envision her invoking spells and calling forth spirits, topped by glowing tresses as she stands in the woods. There's something magical about her, and I wonder why we haven't met before. I wonder again when I find out we live within blocks of each other, and we share a ride home (but that's all). I curl into my pillow and think about her—not my classic dirty fantasies but something else, something calmer, yet no less powerful. I want to float in the ocean with her, go on roller coasters and make brownies with her, spend all night dancing up a storm until we collapse in a happily exhausted heap. I'm not sure how much I want her, and how much I just want her energy, but she has changed my plodding life, and I know I have to see her again.

Sofia must feel the same, because our nights out become fast and frequent. We prowl the neighborhood bars till all hours, digging into each other's life stories like they're the best bowl of ice cream ever. I think about her all the time, send her quick e-mails, plan what I will wear when I see her and look for little gifts to brighten her day. It feels like more than a crush somehow—this is greater than a fleeting feeling that will burn and fade, fast and sharp. This is beyond that schoolgirl flightiness. When I call her, I try not to sound too nervous, but she makes it easy, maybe because she feels the same way. From that first night onward, we are a pair, flitting off into the night, eating edamame well past midnight, and never running out of things to talk about. We are new best friends, but to me she is something more. I don't see anyone else, and don't want to; I just want her, all of her tall, powerful womanliness, and every minute with her feels like a blessing.

I quickly learn that anything can happen when I'm with her; a quiet dinner can become an all-night escapade ending at a stranger's house at 7 A.M. But that's what I like about Sofia— she has such an adventurous spirit, and she brings out mine. Neither of us talks about our present dating situation, so I assume she isn't dating anyone. This way it's easier to lull myself into believing that I can be her girlfriend, and our nights out can continue in the same vein—with a bit of kissing and sex thrown into the mix. I don't consciously think of a plan, a way of letting her know how I feel, because that's too scary. I don't want to shake up our beloved routine, but when I lie awake in bed at night, I know I'm fooling myself when I think that friendship is enough. But I can't risk rejection from a straight best friend again. That's right. It's happened to me before, and it was more painful than anything I'd ever experienced. I can cope with losing a partner, but losing a best friend is just devastating. So I console myself with fantasies and daydreams in which Sofia and I keep each other up long into the night, our lips and tongues and hands roving, probing, and searching until we find all the answers we've ever wanted within each other's bodies.

Still, I can't help taking certain risks. Sometimes, after many, many drinks, I reach out and play with her hair, like I did the very first night. It still feels soft and sensuous, even in the dead of winter when everyone else's hair crackles with split ends. Hers glows, and not just because of its bright color. It's her; she glows in that way that only truly happy people do, like her skin knows she's creatively fulfilled. I find myself immersed in her stories, my own boring days paling in comparison to her outrageous adventures as a film student, gallivanting all over the city to get the perfect shot for her current project. We don't have any mutual friends, so there's nobody I can talk to who will truly understand. I don't want to revert to high-school behavior and confide in any of her friends, though; this is something I'll have to deal with myself. One day I can't wait anymore—suddenly, Sofia is the only thing that matters in my life.

That night, I lie awake until dawn, knowing that I have to find a way to tell her. I search for the precisely perfect wording, the magic phrase that will not only tell her how I really feel, but also make her want me back. I try and try, tossing and turning over words like I'm juggling ice cubes in my mouth. None of them feel right. The next night, I open my mouth repeatedly, letting it hang in the air. Everything I feel for her is so plainly visible, yet impossible to say. I ask for other things— another story, a quarter for the jukebox, a drink. I act out, playing with her hair, flirting with other girls, and seducing her roommate in the middle of the night while Sofia is asleep. Sometimes I think the time to awaken her and touch her has arrived. I want to hold her, to let her wake wrapped in my arms. But she is inscrutable; her big laugh and sparkling eyes tell me she is having fun, but I want to be more than fun to her. Fun is cheap and easy; desire asks for more. I don't want just a quick fling, a casual experiment, a friendship turned affair turned nothing. I want to wake up next to her, to see her shining face at 2 A.M. and 8 A.M. to find the woman under the surface, the one so brimming with life I can barely keep up with her. Again and again, I admire her profile, her attitude, her. And that's how it remains: I watch her from afar.

As many times as I open my mouth, I shut it, afraid of what I might hear in response. I never tell her how I feel; I just stare longingly at her across the room, across the bar, until she is too far away. She moves across the country, and our communication dwindles to an e-mail here, a phone call there. I start to lose track of her vibrant face—her eyebrow ring glinting at me, her big teeth and shining eyes, her glowing hair and aura of excitement. They become hazy memories, until I finally make my way to California. By then, I've almost given up, and of course, the moment I stop trying is the moment my dreams tumble right into my arms.

We spend the evening sipping chocolate martinis and eating sushi as Los Angeles glitters magically. I glance out the restaurant's panoramic window but have eyes only for her. Far removed from Brooklyn's babble, this place feels calm and quiet, serene and perfect. We spend our time staring intently at each other, as she shows me photos from a recent trip to Europe, and immediately she entrances me once again. I let her hazel eyes and animated voice bewitch me.

We step outside afterward, to the ultimate tourist attraction, but one that is surprisingly calm, with no one to interrupt our burgeoning passion. Looking out over a city made suddenly beautiful, its glittering lights illuminating not angels but hills, I let Sofia breathe magic into the gleaming cascade below us. There's Silver Lake, the cool area, there's the valley, there's Hollywood, she tells me, highlighting landmarks as I half-look where her finger points, half-stare at her gorgeous face. And then I take her hand or she takes mine—I don't really remember who does what, but all the months of Brooklyn flirtation have now caught up with us 3,000 miles away. Drunk on vodka and vacation, our tongues tangle. She tastes as perfect as I'd imagined, and I let myself go, relaxing into her strong arms. We don't care about the tourists sweeping around us, or the restaurant employees, and to tell you the truth, as beautiful as our surroundings are, we could be anywhere. Her tongue is warm and spicy, just like her, full of promise and desire. I can't believe that after all those sleepless nights of dreaming about her, of flirting with her landlord and roommate to get closer to her, I have managed to capture her when I am here only fleetingly. But it doesn't matter what sordid circumstances have gotten us together; all that matters is that we are finally sharing the passion I'd felt bubbling up since we first met. I don't wonder why this has only happened now, here, rather than at home, in her bed, where I crashed so many nights and woke up early, staring at her in repose, wishing I could curl up next to her. Asleep, she wasn't quite the same wild child; she lacked the essential vibrancy that came alive in the light of the bar, where she spun tale after entrancing tale.

As usual, after endless making out, squeezing a year's worth of hunger into those kisses, there is no way I can stay. I have to get back to my previous obligations—my family is good at thwarting my chances of getting laid, even when they don't know it. We kiss the sweet, soft, urgent kisses of those who know this will be all they get, who know that kissing isn't simply a prelude. But, oh, is she worth it. Sofia is worth all those nights dreaming and wondering, and she is worth the ones that will come as I imagine ways we might have been together, ways to go back in time and take all we can from each other's bodies. If I could go back in time, I would shove my hand into all that gorgeous, flaming hair, begging it to burn or soothe me, anything to make me feel more alive. We take breaks, slowing down, lingering because we don't want this night to end. We want time to hold still, her arms wrapped around me the way they feel meant to do, as the city continues to gleam and glitter, ours for the taking.

Whenever I wish we'd been able to continue our lust, I pause. Maybe I'm only meant to have those kisses, the ones that linger on my lips years later, the ones that fire me up just as much as her soft hair and animated eyes, the ones that will forever remind me of her. Maybe they are enough to fuel my fantasies, ones that confirm that she will bewitch me from afar for a long, long time. Intentional or not, Sofia has cast her spell on me, and I am grateful to have fallen under it. Maybe she will release me someday, but I'm not in any rush. With her, or even without her, I have all the time in the world as her lingering chocolate kisses keep her in my heart.

touch

●

rachel kramer bussel

"Most profoundly, [sex] is an act of opening up to one another. It is a sharing of energies. It doesn't ask you to be a certain way. It shows you how you are."
—David Guy, *The Red Thread of Passion: Spirituality and the Paradox of Sex*

While I'm inside her, the world stops, and nothing else matters. We are the only people who exist, now or ever. I lose myself as my hands roam her pale skin, and I am completely gone once they reach between her legs, where she is always wet and more than ready. Even for me, sometimes the most talkative girl in the world, words sometimes fail, and this is one of those times. I have very little to say as I spread her open, as I reach literally inside of her, and even though I've done it many times before, and will do so many times again, every time is different and awe inspiring. Each time, it's almost a surprise to find her so eager, so wet she drips and my fingers slide into her as if they were made to fuck her. Each time, it's like a miracle, and in that instant that I enter her, all my doubts and worries slip away, and my life exists in this simple, yet profound, touch.

I always approach her with the best intentions, wanting to expand my horizons, to utilize the vast array of sex toys lying on all sides of me, but tonight, like most nights, I don't really want any of them. My eyes glance at them, but return to the beauty of her cunt, beckoning me. I want—actually I *need*—to feel her for myself, as my fingers coax their way down her body, brushing over her cheek, pressing into her neck, sliding down her chest to dawdle at her nipples, then curving around her hip so my tongue can dance its way along her slightly curved stomach. There is so much of her that asks me to linger, and feeling her impatience only makes me want to prolong things further, until I touch her where she most wants, knowing she will be all the more ready when I get there. I lick the fine hairs of her stomach, pressing my cheek against this softest flesh, until even I can no longer stand the wait. My attempts to tease her have brought me to the edge too.

Sometimes, I watch, looking down as my fingers slip inside her, as she pulls them deeper and sucks me into her. Other times, I lie alongside her and whisper into her ear, tell her what it feels like as I slam my way into her, rough and then gentle, gentle and then rough. Though I spend most of the day thinking about this very moment, once it arrives, I have no plan or map to guide me, only the way she rocks against me and gives me clues in the art of pleasing her.

Time stops, stands still, turns around, remakes itself as we remake ourselves. I have no time to think or process, only the present. I travel by instinct as I lose myself inside her. I shift around, trying to find the most comfortable spot, the place that allows me to touch the most of her skin, not just inside but outside too, where I can feel her warmth and breath and presence. I like to lie lengthwise against her so I can simultaneously touch her head, arm, chest, side, and legs, all the while plunging my fingers inside her. The best part, or one of many best parts about it, is hearing her breath in my ear, a quiet, intimate noise that I miss when my head is not directly next to hers.

Through her breathing, almost more than the wetness surrounding my fingers, I can tell when she is getting closer, approaching that place that we reach alone, together. I live for those moments when I can make her utterly lose control, when the only thing that matters is me pressing into her and her pressing back against me, when the only thing left for her to do is take ragged breaths that seem to catch on themselves, to claw at me in desperation, to bite my arm to show me how much she likes what I'm doing. I want to stay like that forever, even more than I want to make her come, to feel her hot breath on me and sink inside her, toward salvation.

I'm not a religious person, though there have been times when I've moved in that direction. I'm always plagued with too many doubts, logical twists that prevent me from taking that full leap into faith.

And yet, that's exactly how it is. With that same intangible faith that true prayer requires, I seek her out, find new ways to fill the empty spaces inside her, new ways to make her squeeze my hand until I think it will break. I didn't realize until recently how powerful that connection was, perhaps because I'd always had trouble with the concept of faith. I was always the one asking "why?" and "how?" needing proof instead of long-passed-on fables, needing times and dates and names and places to render miracles real. But with her I feel like anything is possible; if I can make her body sing this way, bringing us somewhere we've never been before, over and over again, is that not its own miracle?

I've been the same way about love, not believing that one person could truly do it all for me, that sex could be a communion of sorts rather than a physical act. With her, sex as I knew it, or used to think I knew it, falls away. We reinvent it, and ourselves, over and over again. Sometimes, we spend so many minutes, hours, days lost in our own cocoon, lost in each other's bodies, that I can't function once I leave her. I don't know what to do in the "real world" because she is the only thing that's real to me anymore.

The boys ask me how they should touch a woman, seeking some magic formula that will make them the perfect lovers, bring their girlfriends to surefire orgasms, but I have no idea. When I'm with her, I'm no longer any kind of expert. I barely even know my own name, except when she says it, all deep and throaty and needy. Most of the time, I don't know what I'm doing, don't know where I'm touching her, don't have a technical name for it, or a recalled memory of reading or writing about this. I couldn't, because I've never felt or done anything like this before. With her, I'm not a sexpert but a sorcerer, a magician feeling my way along, teasing, testing, probing, hoping.

Every time I touch her, I do so by instinct. If I were to stop and think about it, I'd be wracked by insecurity, yet with her it all makes perfect sense. She used to say to me, in that breathy, high-on-sex tone, "You know exactly how to touch me," and I thought it was untrue, or an exaggeration. I didn't feel like I knew; it was a happy accident. But maybe my body knew before I did, instinctively. At first, I wasn't sure what to do with her, this sensual, beautiful woman with the body of a girl, thin and seemingly fragile. I didn't know I could put as many fingers as I want inside her, and that she'd eagerly claim them. I didn't know that instead of being fragile, she is infinitely strong; in fact, it's a challenge to break her, to make her shake and shiver and moan, to give some of that strength to me. I didn't know that sliding my fingers inside of her, something as seemingly simple as that, could bring tears to my eyes, making me want to stay there forever. I didn't know that fucking could bring me to the same heights as getting fucked, could make me feel so free and high and happy.

A snapshot: She lies across the queen-size bed, her head hanging off the side, spread out before me like the most delicious buffet. I have been away for a weekend that feels like much longer. I look at her, and it's almost like I've never seen her before. I am nervous and ravenous at the same time, and watching my fingers move over and around her hot pink lips, I shiver, unsure whether to control myself or let go. As I slide my fingers into her, first one then two, and then more, until I have most of one hand pressed deep inside her, I marvel at the way she feels. I touch skin and heat, pressing up against bones and flesh. She asks me what I'm doing to her, and I kiss her because I don't have an answer for her. She is more mysterious than any boy will ever be, holding so many more secrets inside her, ones I live to unearth.

I love that I can bring her so much pleasure by simply turning my wrist this way and that, minute movements that rock her body until I can't stand it anymore and just press as deep as I can. I push and strain, wondering when she will tell me to stop, when she says, "More, deeper," and grabs my wrist and pushes it toward her in a moment of frantic desperation. She lets go, only to claw at me, clutch at me for support lest she fall too far away from this world. I again push my four fingers deep inside and marvel that she can take so much. I push and twist and strain, my own breathing heavy as I sweat while I push, sometimes shaking my whole body back and forth, rocking in unison with her. Even though I'm pressing against her from the inside out, it feels the opposite. I feel like I am pulling her to me, holding on to her from the outside in, taking from her more than giving to her, trying to make sure, even though I know it is impossible, that she will be right here, mine, forever.

With eyes closed and breath frantic, she whispers words

that enter my soul, that stay with me, haunting me late at night as my mind repeats them and my body reacts involuntarily. She tells me secrets and needs and dreams, saying words I don't think I want to hear until they sound so right as they escape her. She tells me I can do whatever I want to her, and suddenly my want expands, racing from simple wishes to a need to consume and devour. An indescribable emotion, something like pride, or lust, or greed, one of those deadly sins we are not supposed to feel, bubbles up, as she lets me touch her everywhere, lets me take us both into uncharted territory. I scare myself a little as her words pump into me, drug-like. My reaction is not what I would have predicted, but nothing about us is what I would have expected.

She is so beautiful, I want to climb inside her, live forever inside her beauty as she continues to open and open and open for me. She makes me want to put my entire self into her, to give her all of me and see what she can do with it, to keep her here, ready and open, just for me, always. Every time she does so, I am in awe of her, of how she can tear me up and twist me around and make me utterly lose myself inside her, of how she makes the art of getting fucked one that requires true passion, discipline and devotion. She is not the kind of girl who lies there and takes it, but one who wrestles with me, verbally and physically, challenging me to push her to new heights, to test my own boundaries, to go deeper, literally and figuratively. I hold one hip, and, with my fingers inside her, rock her whole body, gently at first and then more firmly, watching her breasts jiggle as her cunt tightens around me.

She sucks me into her, drawing me closer and closer until it would be impossible to turn away, even if I wanted to. My thumb massaging her clit makes her spasm involuntarily, pulling me in deeper, and I know she wants more. I look up at her face, wanting to see her eyes before I enter her further, but they are firmly shut, and I close my own for a minute, then slide my other hand inside, palms pressed together as if in prayer. And this is a form of prayer, a form of worshiping something not of this world. Our love, our meeting, our understanding of each other, is not something that was planned, yet it now seems fated. I move my hands slowly, sliding them back and forth, gently coaxing her orgasm from wherever it lurks. I lean my head against her stomach to feel and hear and sense what's happening inside. When it happens, it's like an earthquake, not an eight, but a gently building three, roiling and tumbling as it gathers steam until it finally erupts, lingering longer than it has any right to.

Even when I slide my hands out of her, as slowly as I can, and with great reluctance, I feel her trembling underneath me. Our connection is not severed by the lack of physical contact in that most intimate of places. I pull her toward me and listen to the final shudders that wrack her, and then I pull her closer, and tears fill my eyes. There are no words left for this moment, no way to show or tell her how she can undo me with her trembling, how she intoxicates me. I'm torn between holding her in my arms and kissing her gently, and throwing her back down on the bed, facedown this time, and plunging back into her.

Afterward, I can't stop feeling like a part of me is still with her. For days, my hands are no longer simply my hands; they are beautiful, magical, and all I want to do with them is touch her, again and again. The feeling of being inside her lingers as I type at my keyboard or load my papers into the copier at work, and I marvel that these same hands can perform such mundane tasks alongside such amazing feats. They feel bigger, stronger, as do I.

Our desire for each other is an endless cycle, and just when I think I've had enough, that I am ready to sleep or simply to hold her, she presses against me, darts her tongue out to lick my ear, or tells me something so fabulously dirty I can think

---

only of having her yet again. When we are naked like this, pressed against each other after we've spent all day in bed, life is as perfect as it will ever get.

I never thought the point of religion was to absolve my sins or answer all my questions, yet I felt cheated when my questions could not be answered, the options too intangible for me to fathom. And yet somehow she manages to answer the questions I haven't even asked. Without meaning to, she makes me whole and alive. Naked, she is my angel, my peace offering, everything I will ever need to get by.

When I'm with her, the world stops and nothing else matters. We are the only people who exist, now, or ever. She is my savior, my treasure, my angel. She is the answer to all my prayers, especially the ones I never knew I had.

obsession

●

dr. jane foxx, ph.d.

I am a twenty-nine-year-old devout lesbian. There's never been a doubt about that, or about my resolute need to pursue my desires.

My career as a college professor has allowed me to choose female partners to feed my personal obsession. Indeed, during the past few years, I have been in direct contact with a host of attractive, eager-eyed, female students. A select few of them have been more than willing to join me on a regular basis.

I've always sought the company of other women. I love being with them. I love their touch and feel. I love everything about them!

Please understand, it has always been my intention to settle down with one particular female. However, until recently, I've always been in search of that elusive, ideal companion, and forced to find satisfaction in a series of enjoyable interludes.

Before continuing with this report, I should probably reveal a primary fact about myself, because I don't believe I'm a typical representative of most practicing lesbians. It has to do with specific preferences. In the act of carrying out my primary obsession, I am able to achieve a series of highly satisfying orgasms all on my own, no touching needed!

From what I've read, and have been told by others, this ability is atypical for most women. It has also been difficult for a few of my partners to comprehend. For those women who have raised moderate objections, I have allowed some to return my oral favors in the accepted manner, and it seems to be enough to pacify them, even if I may find it necessary to feign an orgasm or two. Please understand, I do not object to being orally serviced by another female, but my greater preference, by far, is being the active partner.

Most of my female lovers have accepted my explanation, and thoroughly enjoyed themselves by allowing me to repeatedly demonstrate my oral expertise. To date, happily, I have not had any complaints, but rather, a series of sincere compliments, which make my earnest efforts doubly rewarding.

I shall begin this revealing passage with comments about my latest episode of overt oral engagement. Abby Darling is the young beauty's real name. I met the lovely young redhead on a trip to Scotland last summer. My meeting with Abby was like finding an oasis in a desert. The sight and sounds of her lusty awakening stimulated my slumbering desires, and I was overjoyed when our paths crossed.

I've never wanted just any woman, of course. She must be appealing to my inherent instincts; create an irresistible allure in my discerning mind. I hope this description is not too vague for the uninitiated.

I seem to recognize "the lady in question" when we first meet. How do I identify her? That's an excellent question! I shall put it into words for others to ponder.

For myself, I have found blonds can be very nice, but brunets are also special, and redheads, of course, are in a class all their own. I love them all! So, it isn't necessarily the color of the woman's hair that interests me.

The ideal female candidate, who can light the fires of my personal obsession, is around five-foot-six or -seven (about my size). She should be slender, with nicely developed breasts, a winsome figure, and have an attractive appearance. But far more important is the lady's disposition, and her attitude about what is most important in life. In short, is she as lustful as I am about venting her deepest personal desires? I don't believe I should have to convince any woman on this particular point. The lady should already know the depth of her own needs and wants, and be willing to pursue them.

I have met many women who appeared to be absolutely perfect for playing the passive part in our personal activities, but, unfortunately, many of them were not in tune with my obsessive thoughts. Their minds and emotions seemed elsewhere: on business, money matters, college work, weddings, movies, shopping, television, books, and even men.

However, there have been a few vibrantly passionate women along the way who have been more than eager to satisfy my greatest expectations, just as the aforementioned Abby Darling did.

In addition to her natural feminine attributes, Abby was exceedingly desirous for the attention of an experienced female, like me. This fact showed in her revealing behavior. Also, we quickly found the two of us could stand toe-to-toe, naked or not, and appear to be the same height. I like these incidental elements very much! Abby Darling and I were physically and emotionally made for each other!

I first met the Scottish miss after a class at her university, where I'd been invited to be a guest speaker. She lingered afterward, until all the others had departed from the lecture hall. Alone, we quickly found we were immediately attracted to each other. How totally exhilarating our meeting was, right from the beginning!

Abby didn't use the standard compliment I often hear from

others: the trite "I enjoyed your speech very much." No, instead, Abby said to me, "Professor, I think you have the loveliest eyes!"

The novel statement was unexpected, but the flattering words, plus Abby's very feminine image, instantly filled me with that deep down, insistent desire. I already wanted her, and decided to waste no time in declaring my thoughts, especially if she continued to be receptive.

For a moment I was lightheaded, but my mind was nimble enough to come up with an appropriate answer to her comment.

"The better to see you with, my dear," I offered.

In response, Abby returned my smile, introduced herself, and asked if I had time to speak with her at length. Of course, I was fully agreeable. We shook hands warmly, and I suggested we have lunch together.

As Abby and I left the building, our conversation was not about English composition (my specialty), as I thought it would be. Rather, we were forced to concentrate on a sudden, horrendous downpour, our lack of umbrellas, and the wisdom of hurrying to Abby's nearby living quarters to seek refuge from the troubling weather.

That was how Abby and I first found ourselves alone. In this manner, the unexpected rainstorm turned out to be a splendid blessing in disguise.

Abby and I were drenched before we reached her door, so removing our wet outer garments was a sheer necessity. Abby graciously gave me a robe to wear while our clothes had a chance to dry. She slipped into a silky dressing gown, and made us some hot tea. A fine beginning!

I watched Abby Darling flit about the kitchen, and admired her figure, while she began asking me questions. "How much longer will you be in Europe, professor?" Abby inquired.

"I have another three weeks of free time before I have to

return to the U.S. to begin my new classes."

"And what will you do during that three weeks?"

"I have nothing definite planned," I told her. "I thought I might do some touring of the continent, perhaps."

"Why don't you stay here with me for a while?" Abby offered. "I'm sure the two of us could find lots to do together. I only have a few classes during the coming weeks, but the rest of the time I'm free, and…"

"Are you interested in me, Abby Darling?" I blatantly asked.

"Yes, I suppose I am!"

"I hope it's in a romantic sense!"

"I feel it is," she replied breathlessly.

"How intriguing. Can you tell me why?"

"I don't know why, professor," Abby said. "There's just something about you I find utterly fascinating. It's your accent, your looks, your figure, your wonderful eyes, something. I'm not exactly sure, but I like what I see and hear very much."

"Goodness, what a wonderful compliment!" I stepped forward to give Abby Darling an appreciative hug. Her total, sweet-smelling femininity felt wonderful in my hungry arms.

The initial embrace between us lingered, and I offered, "I must tell you, Abby Darling, I'm the one who usually does such deliberate propositioning."

"Oh, were you going to proposition me, professor?" Abby smiled coyly.

"If the opportunity presented itself, at the proper moment I'm sure I would have, Darling, but you've already taken it upon yourself to do the honors."

"Is that OK with you, professor?" Abby asked.

"Of course, and I feel I just might accept the offer to stay with you for a while."

"Charmed, professor!"

"Delighted, Darling!" I smiled.

A moment later, the intriguing Scottish miss and I initiated a token kiss. I regarded it as a simple gesture to seal our spoken agreement. However, it did not turn out to be a gentle smooch; it quickly developed into a "zinger," with plenty of full-bodied, clutching pressures between both of us, from top to bottom!

That initial kiss thrilled both of us to our toes. Abby's tongue had met mine, creating a swirling delight, and I instantly realized I had found a female college student of great promise. Abby knew exactly what she wanted, just as I did! How delightful!

However, there was a brief moment of tentativeness, when Abby whispered nervously, her lips near my ear, "I've never done anything like this before, professor."

I saw Abby Darling needed encouragement. I gave it quickly.

"You'll do just fine, Darling, I promise! It's what you need, and it's what we both want!"

Less than a minute later, after the phone was removed from the hook, with little coaxing, other than my oblique description of my lusty intentions, Abby Darling slipped out of her dressing gown. What a kick it was to have the preliminaries go so quickly, and so easily!

What I remember most about Abby disrobing was the fascinating curvature of her lithe body (upper and lower), especially in her cute, dainty underthings. I became quietly mesmerized, as her robe whisked completely away.

I try not to miss the slightest detail of such beginnings. To my educated eye, Abby Darling looked quite appetizing. Yes, I think *appetizing* is the correct word. I felt as a famished woman might in seeing an appealing delicacy before her hungry eyes. Simply by being there, the dear girl made me want her very badly!

A great prerequisite in spurring my interest is in the way the lady in question presents herself. I thought Miss Abby Darling's deportment was ideal, and, if she could be believed, she was a virgin at that! How absolutely exhilarating!

As the ultraprovocative scene unfolded, I vividly remember Abby's lace-trimmed panties, and the way the filmy material clung to her lower body. I suppose a male in my position would have had drooling lips and a throbbing erection at this point, but it wasn't a male facing the delightful Abby Darling. It was me: a desirous female treated to a superb, female attraction.

I recall watching Abby move through the simple act of hanging her robe back in the closet. The picturesque scene left very little to the imagination, and I wondered how many other lesbians miss such fleeting visual treats? I try not to!

Abby Darling noticed my fixed gaze on her, and she spoke with a smile. "It was your eyes and your speaking voice that first attracted me, professor, but I must also say, you have the most fascinating lips too."

In response, I felt it was the perfect time to offer, "The better to eat you with, my dear!"

Abby laughed with undisguised appreciation. She unashamedly winked, while murmuring, "Ooh, I can hardly wait, professor!" That caused more anxious smiles between us. My restless tongue was simply aching to begin its studied debauchery of this sweet young miss, and I had just told her so, as plainly as I thought necessary.

Holding Abby in my arms after another passionate kiss had concluded, I said to her, "Something tells me you're going to be absolutely delicious, young lady!"

"I certainly hope so!" Abby smiled. "I feel I've been waiting for you a long, long time, professor, but would you like to take a shower first?"

"Did you take one this morning?"

"Yes, of course," she said. "I always do, but I thought you might like to…"

"I really don't think it's necessary, Darling," I assured her, hoping my burgeoning anxiety wasn't too overly apparent. "Perhaps we'll take a shower together, later."

"As you wish, professor." Abby grinned through her nervousness. "I guess I'm ready. Are you?"

"Of course," I answered with a lingering smile. I was delighted that we already understood each other's basic motives and mutual desires. Less than an hour had elapsed since we first met; we were making marvelous progress.

Whether our coming together set a record for brevity, I don't know, but I've always believed wasting time about such fundamental matters is pure foolishness. If both women want to experience each other, I say go for it, just as Abby and I did!

Incidentally, Abby called me "professor" throughout our relationship, and I liked hearing her use the word. Since she was still a college student, the title seemed to fit the circumstances, and it lent a charming atmosphere to our promising liaison.

In return, I referred to Abby as "Darling," which was her genuine family name. But the word had a dual effect.

For example, when I implored, "Remove your bra and panties, Darling," Abby looked at me closely to determine if my saying the word was an order, or a term of endearment. We both got a kick out of such playful double entendre. Our minds were truly in tune!

"As you wish, professor," Abby replied, accompanied with a flirtatious smile, and a mock salute, which caused both of us to playfully laugh again.

Abby turned away from me to unfasten her flowered bra, and I got to watch her nimble fingers do routine feminine things she had obviously done thousands of times before, yet it was a beautiful sight. I was certain few, if any, had ever viewed such a scene with Abby Darling before. I felt singularly honored.

I was still gazing at the fascinating attractiveness of Abby's exposed breasts when her two thumbs hooked into the waistline of those sheer panties, whisking and wiggling them away from her lovely body. Now, I could see all of Abby's enticing, natural beauty. She stood on her toes to teasingly pirouette before me. What a picture she made! Such inviting scenes will always be imprinted deeply in my lusty lesbian mind.

In another moment, a warm and naked Abby Darling was in my anxious arms, inviting me to kiss her again, and to touch any portion of her unclothed beauty. Holding and caressing her became my chief interest, but it was only the beginning of the exciting activity that followed.

As if I were a movie director, I had Abby semirecline before me on the comfortable couch in her living room. Two soft pillows went beneath her head. I also placed a towel under her shapely rear end: It is one of my personal idiosyncrasies to be as neat as possible during such intimate revels.

An expectant Abby Darling was fully naked (except for her earrings), and I still wore my robe, as I knelt on the floor before her. Soon, I was kissing here and there, from top to bottom, across the front of her lovely body. What a true, giddy pleasure it was!

I should say a word about bodily positions. There are many poses two lusting women can assume in practicing the unparalleled delights of oral sex. I prefer the passive female to be lounging slightly, as Abby was, on a couch. My position is on the floor between her slender thighs. This gives both principals the chance to exchange occasional words and glances during any of the romantic action to follow. A fully reclining female, flat on a mattress, can't see much and misses half the fun, in my opinion. Besides, I like being watched as the encounter proceeds. Knowing the passive lady's attention is fully on me is a pure kick like no other. Does this mean I'm an exhibitionist about my oral craft? Probably!

My mind was in a delicious whirl, mostly from Abby's reactions to my bold, studied attempt to fully awaken her natural desires. She was already softly sighing with undisguised excitement as my kisses began contacting the most sensitive parts of her body. She was, as I suspected she would be, totally luscious!

After Abby's delectable mouth had been soundly kissed, her inviting nipples came to my attention. I showered them with many licks and loud, sucking kisses just to hear Abby sigh and moan so rapturously. Afterward, the wondrous trail of my lips led southward, across her sleek abdomen, and my face moved inevitably toward the juncture of her thighs.

Shortly, at my continuing direction, Abby's lovely legs came up and apart, with me nestled between them. One of her feet came to rest on a convenient coffee table, which allowed me easy access to my ultimate target. But I paused for a moment to study the intriguing sight before me.

Truly, I consider myself an unabashed connoisseur on the subject of vaginas, having viewed and dabbled with my share. Abby Darling's was a classic edition, with those luscious parts of tender female flesh surrounded by a bevy of tight pubic curls. It was, and is, a lovely sight for these eager eyes to behold.

My personal oral technique begins by slowly blowing gentle wisps of warm breath against the exposed parts of the outer vagina. This subtle but very effective action is designed to bring the passive lady's emotions to an instant simmer.

Accordingly, Abby Darling responded with more distinct moaning and a slight, undulating motion of her lower body.

Prolonged and pleasurable sighs escaped her open mouth.

To my trained ear, it was as if Abby Darling was already in pure ecstasy.

This is the kind of response an adventurous lesbian adores hearing. I was certain we were headed down a blissful path together!

When my happy tongue finally touched Abby's most sensitive flesh, it was as if she had contacted an external energy source. She was instantly ecstatic.

Unmistakable sounds of erotic joy came from Abby Darling's lips. This response was greeted by several more of my most skillful licks and kisses. I believed both of us were close to orgasms of unequaled proportions!

Indeed, a few moments later, Abby Darling obviously began an excited climax. She humped against my obliging mouth as if wanting more and more! Right on cue, my own unique style of orgasming was unleashed at nearly the same moment. On a standard scale of one to ten, I would have given us both a fifteen! Really!

In retrospect, I'm certain that if Abby and I had been entered together in an Olympic event, we would have surely taken the gold medal in the cunnilingus category. In my creative mind, I could see the two of us standing on the podium at the games, taking the thunderous cheers from the adoring crowd of onlookers.

I was absolutely delighted for the sweet, young miss, plus my own success at setting us both off with such quaking exuberance. Abby Darling was joyfully delirious, and I was kind enough to let her bask in a personal afterglow before thinking of going on. We both needed a few moments to recover from the heights of our success. Fondling her was a distinct pleasure, which allowed me to experience the wondrous moment's total enjoyment.

Very soon, I blew more wisps of warm breath against Abby's tingling flesh to further titillate her awakened senses. She squirmed lustily with each rush of caressing air. This led me to believe we could not rest on the laurel of winning one single "Olympic event." The championship medal had to be defended, and for that to happen, the two of us had to continue our diligent practice. These were the entertaining thoughts that filled my creative mind during our time together!

I fed Abby Darling a fresh, openmouthed kiss on the moist spot of her deepest desires. As I'd hoped, the lingering kiss (with renewed tonguing action) reignited her fires of passion, and she bid me to go on. I was doubly delighted.

I knew this was the moment to introduce the tip of one manicured and educated finger into the mix. Very gently, I penetrated the wrinkled folds of Abby's personal desire. In response, I heard a fresh cascade of appreciative sighs and moans from her trembling mouth. I had struck a raw, excitable nerve within her. She quaked anew with great delight! I was enthralled with my success!

My penetrating finger soon became two, and I used them both to thrust deeply against the tireless motion of Abby's lower body. She soon squealed her unleashed ecstasy about another huge orgasm.

Afterward, my delighted college student was in my arms. She clung to me for a long while, waiting until her emotions had returned to a more stable level.

As she glowed in my embrace, I dutifully explained to Abby Darling there was no need to return the oral favors I had lovingly bestowed on her. "I'm sure there will be plenty of other opportunities for us both in the near future," I told her.

"I hope so," she murmured through moist lips.

Indeed, I had experienced two of my own exciting, highly satisfying orgasms, while Abby was enjoying her own.

So, there was no need to do more than to bask in our mutual contentment.

Accordingly, Abby Darling made room for me to lie with her on the couch, where we hugged and kissed for a long while, enjoying each other's warm company.

"You're wonderful, professor," Abby blissfully murmured.

"Did I play you like a violin?" I asked.

"You certainly did, professor," Abby replied, amid several soft kisses to my appreciative face. Such a marvelous experience for us both, I thought.

That was the beginning of a heady romance. During the

next three weeks, we baked cookies, did some shopping, saw a couple of theater plays, took several photos, went sightseeing, and enjoyed ourselves together immensely.

Abby Darling and I also made a few tentative plans for the future. As soon she graduated, in a few more months, Abby would make an effort to join me at my university in the U.S., perhaps as a new teacher. In addition, we made plans to see each other during spring break, three months ahead. For both of us, it was a small consolation, but one we would eagerly anticipate.

Time, it is said, waits for no one, and all too soon my plane was scheduled to leave, taking me back to my duties as a college professor. I knew I would never forget how my abiding obsession had brought me into the eager arms of Abby Darling. I hoped we would meet again.

a day in the park

●

heather towne

Last summer, I visited my Auntie Elizabeth in Winnipeg, Canada for a couple of weeks. She showed me the sights, such as they are—the Forks, old St. Boniface, various museums, etc.—and one sunny Sunday I went by myself to Assiniboine Park to see the zoo and conservatory. After doing that, I stretched out on the big lawn in front of the pavilion building to soak up some moody Manitoba sunshine.

I was lying on my beach towel, staring up at the big, blue, cloudless prairie sky, wearing nothing more than a white halter top, a pair of pink shorty-shorts, and a coating of suntan lotion, when a couple of friendly girls asked me if I wanted to throw a Frisbee around. I said, "Sure!"

We started tossing the plastic disc back and forth. The two chicks were both around my age, but judging from the various tattoos and piercings they sported, they lived wild lives; they were the kind of girls my mother would have never let me befriend in high school.

We took a break after a half hour, and Lynn and Sandy invited me to park my towel on their prime patch of greenery—in the sun, behind some bushes to one side of the

Pavilion. Well, we gals got to talking, and yup, you guessed it, to rubbing.

"Looks like you could use s'more oil, Katy," Lynn said, cradling a tube of sunscreen in her hand. She was a tall, lean skater girl, with bright blue eyes and long black hair loosely braided into twin ponytails. Her body was plastered with all sorts of tattoos, blatantly visible thanks to the tube top and cutoffs she was wearing. Her jutting nipples almost poked holes in her top's thin material.

"Never can get enough of the good stuff," I quipped, rolling over onto my stomach, inviting Lynn to lay on some lotion.

"I got your back," she said, crawling over to me on her knees and squeezing a dollop of cool, white goop onto my shoulders.

I rested my chin on my hands and murmured appreciatively as the SuicideGirl look-alike rubbed cream into my upper body in slow, soothing strokes.

"Need some help, girlfriend?" Sandy asked, playfully pushing Lynn aside and putting her hot little hands on my slippery, sun-kissed skin. Sandy was short and blond, with green eyes and a slightly chubby body. Her orange tie-top was taxed to the max, trying to contain her plump, round titties. Both girls had purple tongue studs and silver belly button rings, and while Sandy only had a few tattoos compared to Lynn's colorful body-art collage, two nipple rings showed through her top.

"Hey, let's share!" Lynn yelped at Sandy, and then knelt in front of my face, her clothed cunny millimeters away from my nose. She leaned over and rubbed up and down my back, as Sandy straddled my ankles and rubbed my legs, using the same slow, sensual technique.

Well, what with the blazing sun, the desert-hot air, and the girl's caressing hands and probing fingers, my cunny was soon sweating as heavily as the rest of my body, getting ticklish with wetness. And my clitty-senses really started tingling when

Sandy began openly plying my butt cheeks, sliding her greasy hands underneath my shorts and kneading my taut ass. Lynn took that as her cue to jam her cunny right into my face, and I got a good, wet whiff of the babe's obvious dampness. She slipped her fingers right under my top and rubbed away, easing her hands down my squished titties' bare sides, copping a good feel.

"You like, Katy?" she asked, as Sandy dive-bombed her slippery digits in between my bronzed pillows and probed my pucker.

"Yeah!" I gasped, my mouth full of the girl's shorts.

"It'll feel even better on the flip side," Sandy giggled, and the two wicked wenches rolled me over and felt me up where it really counted.

Lynn pushed my top down and unabashedly glad-handed my naked titties, gripping and squeezing them, my nipples swelling to instant erection in the open air. She pinched and primped my rosy-red buds, rolled them between her long, slender fingers, her thighs straddling my head. Sandy unbuttoned my shorts and pulled them down and off, pushed my legs open, and danced her fingers along my inner thighs, right up to my dripping cunny, lightly caressing my silken folds.

Now that everything was out in the open, so to speak, I decided to give the horny honeys what they obviously wanted. After all, I wanted it too! I spread my legs wider, allowing Sandy to get serious with her internal body massage, then reached up and unfastened Lynn's cutoffs. She quickly peeled them off, and I mashed my lips against her glistening pink girlie-lips and tongued the silver ring that pierced the top of her labes.

"Fuck, yeah!" Lynn screamed.

I gripped her tight, round butt cheeks and licked excitedly at her delightfully shaven snatch. She was wetter than Lake Manitoba, and she tasted sweet and tangy.

"The girl's a natural!" Sandy exclaimed, diving onto her stomach between my legs and spreading my cunny flaps with her fingers, dipping her tongue into my honey pot.

I lapped at Lynn's cunny, fumbling her cunt ring around on the tip of my tongue as she played with my boobies, fondling them like crazy. Then she leaned forward and started rubbing my buzzer, and I almost came buckets right then and there, with Sandy tonguing my snatch and Lynn fingering my love button. But, somehow, I managed to hold off my orgasm and keep right on licking Lynn's tasty slit.

It was Lynn that went off first, screaming, "Fuck! I can't take it anymore!" As she buffed my clitty in a frenzy, her light-ly muscled body jerked with orgasm. I frantically lapped at her conch, and she was jolted again and again with ecstasy. She drenched my face in hot, sticky come, and it was all I could do to keep from drowning. Desperately, I swallowed as much girl juice as I could.

And just when Lynn had almost calmed down, I exploded like a sexual firecracker. Sandy pumped her tongue in and out of my pink, diddling me with her tongue stud, while Lynn's thumb became a blur on my clitty, and my cunny tingled out of control. A giant, wet orgasm welled up and tidal-waved through my body, flooding Sandy's mouth.

"Mmmm," I moaned, my mouth still buried in Lynn's poon. I thrashed around on the towel in a virtual seizure, coming with a blistering intensity that shocked even me. Those two lezzies knew how to work a babe into a lather, let me tell you!

When Lynn and I had recovered from our girlie joy, we immediately went to work on big-titted, baby-fatted Sandy, laying her flat on my towel and each grabbing one big, brown boob. We felt up her hot, heavy knockers, licked and sucked her outrageously distended mocha nipples, and pulled on her gold nipple rings with our teeth like we were going to tear them right off her jugs. She could only grip our bobbing heads and whimper with pleasure.

Lynn and I gave that squirming, curvy girl some sweet, sweet titty loving before I boldly licked my way down her voluptuous body, tongue-tickled her belly button stud for a moment, and then slid my tongue into her juicy cunny. Lynn stayed latched to her girlfriend's fat, pierced nipples, as I parted Sandy's damp, sun-ripened pussy lips with my tongue and dove deep into her pink.

"Yeah! Eat me, Katy!" the buxom, bronzed blond hollered, oblivious to the crowd of sun worshippers just beyond our shrub-walled sanctuary.

I waggled my tongue inside the undulating girl's sex hole, fucking her with my hardened pink spear. Then I pinched her clitty with my fingers and sealed my sticky lips around it, sucking hard. Sandy bucked up and down on the beach towel, Lynn mouth-riding her jiggling titties, me wet-vaccing her swollen clitty.

"I'm coming!" the tag-teamed hottie shrieked, just before she squirted—and I mean squirted—directly into my face.

I got more than a mouthful of Sandy's liquid sunshine, as she sprayed goo over and over. Finally, she blasted one last geyser into my face, leaving her cunny empty. Lynn lifted my head up from her girlfriend's soaking snatch and kissed me, and then the two of us Frenched hungrily, passing Sandy's sticky goodness back and forth between us.

And by the time I finally exited sun- and come-drenched Assiniboine Park, I was mentally and physically burned to a crisp.

try me

●

ana martinez

All night, I'd been staring at this one particular girl, who in her complete and utter beauty, stood out like the moon among stars. Because this was L.A., where everyone glittered to some extent, shining a grace out into the world so bright it beamed across TV screens everywhere, I'd become inured to it over the years, the glamour now nothing but an extra layer to float through. Instead of the usual tanned blond who crossed my path—her teeth a perfect white, her body a perfect size two, everything absolutely perfect—Raquel was different. Her skin was naturally darker than any fake tan, her black hair gleaming in the light. Her lips were red and glossy, though they were the kind that would have looked gorgeous totally bare. I moved across the room as if by magic, knowing I had to meet her. I wasn't even sure why I'd come out to this same dyke bar every week, looking for love, or at least a momentary connection. There were never any girls like me, ones who weren't from here and were proud of it; all the other dark-skinned girls seemed intent on becoming just like the blonds, complete with highlights and fake laughs. Yes, even the dykes. But Raquel was different; she knew she could stop traffic, and held court at the bar while women swirled around her.

I moved to join them, whispering to the bartender to find out her name, and her drink. I looked decent, respectable, butcher than anyone there, but only just so in dark jeans and a plain white top, my short hair hanging to my shoulders. No makeup, but a small ring on my pinkie finger. I had a matching one at home, had had it in my bedside drawer ever since Laura returned it to me. I walked over to Raquel with the glass of white wine, and as if by magic, the crowds seemed to part, and then she looked at me. I set the glass in front of her, and she smiled, a real smile, one that seemed to move straight through my body.

She grabbed my hand, and I was surprised by how soft yet strong hers was. Her fingers felt like she slathered them in lotion all day, every day, so feminine and delicate, yet her grip was fierce and determined as she took my fingers into hers, stroking along my palm with those short, strong nails. She took my hand like that was all she needed to do for me to be hers, and she was right. I let her, offered myself to her there at that very moment, docile and hungry for more. Then, though I'd never done such a thing before in my life, I took her hand in mine and kissed it, softly and gently. She wrapped those luscious fingers around my head and pulled my head close to hers. "Meet me outside in twenty minutes," she whispered, before darting her tongue into my ear, causing my knees to almost buckle. I had no idea what was in store, but it would have been impossible to resist this command.

Somehow, I managed to wait the requisite time, and when I walked outside, her head was poking out of a gorgeous white limo. I hadn't seen her leave, but then again, my head had been slightly muddled by her sweet words, and my hand was still tingling from her touch. She pulled me into her limo and then those glistening lips were upon mine. The driver whisked us off, somewhere, while she plundered me like we'd been doing this all our lives. She put her whole self into the kiss, holding nothing back, and even though we officially knew nothing more than each other's names, kissing her felt like coming home. Her beauty, so exotic set against the bar's backdrop, was perfect here as those juicy lips claimed mine. It felt like a movie, or a dream, and before I could even have a chance to feel splotchy and pale in comparison to her smooth lusciousness, she had laid me out across the backseat. She treated me like such a goddess that I became one, right there in her arms, as her magic fingers slowly undressed me. It felt like time was moving in slow motion, until her tongue reached my panties. Then, everything sped up like a roiling roller coaster as she licked my folds between the fabric, her tongue hot and spicy. She bit my thigh, nipping at the tender flesh there, and then used her fingers again to tap against my pussy. I jerked against her when she did this, practically gushing all over the seat. "Yes, please," was all I managed to get out, but she understood.

I was used to being the butch, the quiet stud who got her girls off, who watched proudly as her own fingers slid inside the latest girl, watching her quiver and quake, but something always stopped me from letting them return that pleasure. Nerves and long-held fears would rise to the surface, but now this gorgeous stranger had managed to go where so many valley girls before her had failed. I could see her shiny hair gleaming in the light streaming through the window, her perfectly plump ass, encased in flowing black layers, sticking up as she angled her tongue so it slid right inside me. She worked me expertly, flicking up and down, to the sides, plunging her tongue inside me, then coming back out to lavish my clit with attention, and I held tightly onto anything I could, my hands squeezing the seat, the door handle, banging against them when the sensations got too much. She reached that moment where I usually paused, froze up, and started over, but she kept going. She knew exactly what she was doing to me as she shoved two of those smooth, perfect fingers into my pussy while her lips wrapped around my clit and didn't let go. The dual assault left me absolutely breathless. I closed my eyes and savored her touch, felt what she was giving me; not just her lips and fingers, an explosive orgasm, but herself. For me, sex can so often seem like an exercise in mutual masturbation, each person just biding their time until they get off, with little effort made to truly connect. I'd had too many relationships like that, and yet this exotic stranger seemed to be giving all of herself to me. I imagined her naked, floating on her back in a pool of gleaming water, parting her pussy lips with her fingers while I watched, and then she added another finger, quickly, those tiny invaders pressing urgently against every throbbing part of my cunt. I came then, shuddering against her, grinding my teeth as I tried not to squeeze my legs around her face. She stayed down there, licking me slowly, pulling out as if it were the last thing on earth she wanted to do.

When she rose she moved up to kiss me, then methodically stuck one finger at a time into her mouth, sucking my juices off each one. I had so many questions I wanted to ask her— Who are you? Where are we going? Why me?—but I just stared at her. She was like me in some ways, both of us Hispanic, the traces of an accent rolling off our tongues, both looked at with some confusion when we walked into a queer setting. And yet that was all I imagined we had in common; her kind of beauty, whatever her background, doesn't come along every day. She brushed a stray strand of hair off my face and stared into my eyes, hers wide and brown and soulful. "Carida," she whispered, lightly tracing her fingers along my cheek. "Come home with me," she said, as we pulled into a driveway.

I wasn't sure what was happening. I didn't meet girls with limos that often, but that wasn't even what made me hesitate. She was too perfect, too special, too out-of-this-world for the likes of little old me. I'd gotten used to my life, solid and singular as it was, had given up on glitz, glamour, and, most of all, love soon after moving to the City of Angels. I looked back at her, unsure of how to tell her why I couldn't come in. She seemed to read my hesitation. "Try me," she said quietly, her gaze boring into mine. So when she got out, walked around the car, opened my door, and held out her hand, I took it. As crazy as it sounds (even to me), I've been trying her ever since.

first kiss

●

amie m. evans

The first person I kissed was the girl next door. It was the
longest courtship in lesbian history. When her family first
moved into the neighborhood, she told everyone her name
was Steve. We were six years old at the time. I set my hair in
long Shirley Temple curls, and my mother dressed me in skirts
or elastic-waist pants with ruffly shirts with ribbons. Steve
lived in jeans, and her long dirty-blond hair hung about her
shoulders, always needing to be brushed. She didn't look like a
boy, or like me. She sat with her legs apart, and moved through
space in a way that seemed foreign and exciting. She didn't
have dolls, and her room wasn't painted pink, unlike all the
other girls I knew. She had balls, bats, and gloves for games I
didn't even know existed. She was the only girl in my white
middle-class small-town neighborhood who rode a boys' bike.
I called her Steve even after I knew her real name was Pam. She
liked it, and I liked pleasing her.

At eight, we played house in the metal shed in my backyard. I served her milk in small plastic pink cups with roses
painted on them, and cookies on matching pink plastic plates.
She brought me flowers picked from the neighbors' front

yards. We made up conversations mimicking the adults around us. She complained about a hard day at work; I gave detailed descriptions of clothing I'd purchased that day, friends I'd had lunch with, gossip I'd heard, and places I'd like to visit on our next vacation. We pushed my cat around the neighborhood in a doll stroller, holding hands, pretending the cat was our new baby.

The winters that we were eight and nine, we played space games in the snow. Bundled in our snowsuits, we pretended we were space travelers stranded on some uncharted planet's icy moon. We built snow fortresses, and snow walls to protect our fortresses, pretending our lives depended on sticking together. We stockaded ourselves with snowballs to defend our safe house against attacks by her younger brothers, the planet's hostile native population. Again and again, I was taken prisoner by the natives and she rescued me.

We took our sleds to the hillside near our homes, and I clasped my arms and legs around Steve. I told her not to go too fast, not to go too close to the trees. I told her I was afraid. She told me to hold on, not to worry or be frightened, and launched us down the hill at the trees, announcing we were going faster than we had ever gone before. I screamed, clung tighter, and squealed with delight as I hid my face in the back of her nylon down-stuffed coat. When the sled stopped I protested that she had done it on purpose to scare me, my heart racing from the thrill. She promised not to do it again, mockingly begging my forgiveness, and then she coaxed me into going down an even bigger hill. We pretended the sled was a motorcycle, like the one the older boy up the street had, or an out-of-control spaceship. We sailed down the hill, through the trees, sometimes tipping over, sometimes making it safely out the other side, and sometimes crashing head-first into a tree.

When the cold got to be too much and our clothes grew too

wet, we went back to my house and made real hot cocoa with milk and whipped cream. We sat in my room in our T-shirts and long underwear, and I rubbed Steve's feet until they were warm. I rubbed her back and the small, developing bulges in her arms. I sat straddled across her butt—two innocent school-girls. Neither of our parents questioned or suspected what was building between us. Neither of us suspected it either.

At ten, Steve beat up the neighborhood boys at my behest. Sometimes I had her beat them up because they teased, taunt-ed, or shoved me, but just as often I had no reason aside from wanting her to do it. I liked the idea of her pounding some boy's face in defense of a perceived wrong to my invented honor. With tears in my eyes, sometimes from true assaults and sometimes conjured by inflicting pain on myself, I feigned helplessness. I spilled the details of real and created injustices, showing her any marks, and forcing my bottom lip out in a soft pout. I acted surprised as I hurried behind Steve, asking where she was going as she stomped after the boy I had accused.

Standing just close enough to see her muscles tighten as her fist made contact with a boy's face or stomach, just close enough to hear her fist connect with flesh and bone, I watched her humiliate whatever boy I had accused, who was inevitably weaker than she. I saw blood and heard the boy beg for her mercy, which only I, ultimately, could grant: To answer to his pleas, Steve always turned to me. A nod of my head, and he was forced to apologize, then freed; a shake, and she would continue to torture him. She was my Lancelot, but I was not Guinevere. I was Morgan, hiding in an illusion, presenting myself as sweet Guinevere and savoring each moment of the battle, disappointed only by the fact that I could not actively participate.

At twelve, I got a bra and my period. By that point the boys had long stopped coming near me; they crossed the street to avoid me, afraid of what I would tell Steve. In the summer Steve and I lay in the grass on the hills by our houses, her head in my lap. I read aloud from *Dracula, Frankenstein,* or *The Book of Martyrs,* stopping to spoon raspberry sherbet into her mouth, or run an ice cube over her neck and upper arms. I ran my fingers through her hair as I read. Steve rolled onto her side, pushing her face against my stomach, requesting that I reread sections she liked. Eventually, she playfully pushed me onto my back and wrestled with me, always letting me believe I was winning. Inevitably, to my delight, she climbed on top of me and pinned my wrists, threatening some horrible treatment and tickling me, rolling us, linked together, down the side of the hill, releasing me as we both laughed.

I put my head on Steve's shoulder or chest and she wrapped her arm around me. Her fresh, clean sweat filled my nose, mixing with the smells of the earth and summer and grass. Our laughter stopped, our breathing slowed to normal, and, in silence, I reached an arm across her to feel the bulge of the young newly developed muscles in her upper arm. My head still on her chest, I traced with one nail, then two flat fingertips, the curve of each muscle as she tightened then relaxed it. She pulled me closer to her, running her free hand over my developing hips. Steve's small breasts disappeared as she lay on her back. The lines of her body seemed to have stayed the same from early childhood—her hips barely there, her thighs slim, muscular. My body seemed to be reforming itself, shifting inward at my waist, out at the hips and chest. Her hands touched the curves of my hips, my waist, the small protrusion of my lower stomach, and the soft curve of my upper arm and shoulder. My fingers ran over the smooth flatness of her stomach and the tight, compact lines of her hips and thighs.

Our breathing grew heavier. I thought about lifting my head, looking up into her face. I imagined Steve leaning down and kissing me, like boys did in movies. Her hand strayed to the curve of my ass and to the bare flesh of the back of my thigh. I froze, stopped stroking her arm, stopped breathing, and concentrated on lifting my face toward hers, but I was paralyzed by the warmth of her hand on my suddenly cold flesh, by the tingling between my legs, and the silence that seemed to engulf us. We lay there for an eternity, my head fixed to her chest, her hand cupped just under my ass, her other hand gripping my shoulder as if to hold me up, preventing me from falling or rolling away. My fingertips pressed against the upper muscle of that arm, supporting it as it supported me. Our breathing was heavy, rhythmic; our hearts raced in excitement, fear.

Then, from somewhere deep in the silence, Steve flipped me over onto my back, straddled me, pinned my arms to the grass, and looked into my eyes, the full weight of her body concentrated on her pelvic bone, pressed against mine. I wanted her to kiss me. I wanted to know what being kissed by her felt like. She released my arms, shifted her weight to her knees, and announced she was hot and wanted to go home to go swimming. On the way home we rode single file, not talking or racing. I shifted my body against the bike seat, rubbing my clit against the hard frame under the padding, wanting to touch between my legs but being unable to do so.

At night we swam in the pool with only the deck lights on. The water away from the deck looked murky and dark, our silhouettes barely visible. Steve wore a T-shirt over her one-piece bathing suit, and I sported a bikini. On nights like these Steve always splashed around, jumping off the deck, diving into the dark water, and grabbing at my ankles. Silently, she would swim up behind me and emerge from the water, lifting me into the air and tossing me, pulling down my bottoms or lifting up my top, exposing my new breasts or my recently sprouted pubic hair. I would pretend to be outraged and feign modesty. Night after night I climbed out of the pool, wrapping a towel around myself and sitting on the deck with my feet in the water, pouting and ignoring Steve's show of aquatic ability. Steve always lifted herself onto the deck next to me, put her arm around me, pulled my resistant body close to hers, and cooed and coaxed me back into the pool.

We would both get into the center of a giant donut tube, facing each other, and float around in the darkness, our legs entangled and rubbing each other under the water. An occasional knee rubbed briefly against a crotch as we floated, our arms hooked on the tube's dry top. I put my head on her shoulder and wrapped my arms around her neck; she put her arms around my lower back, supporting our buoyant bodies with her upper arms on the tube. Steve pulled me close, our small breasts touching, our legs entangled, lightly brushing each other's crotches. Silent. Nervous. Excited. We floated calmly in the tube, protected by the dark still night.

Sometimes Steve's hand would slip down the back of my bikini bottoms and cup the wet tight young flesh of my ass. Her hand would circle around to trace the line of newly developed pubic hair. She tugged lightly at my bottoms, pulling them down to explore my lower body under the cover of the water, in the safety of the dark. She brushed her fingers over my pubic hairs but never went any further. She never separated the fleshy lips, or explored what was hiding in the new forest. The whole world seemed to hold its breath, waiting to see what would happen next.

I always waited for the spotlight to come on from the house, knowing that if our parents saw us like this, collapsed in an embrace in the tube, we would be in trouble for some reason I didn't understand, but still I knew there would be trouble. When the light came on—as it always did—Steve released me; I slipped underwater and silently emerged, with my bottom back in place, across the pool(as far as one breath would allow me to swim under the water. Steve and I never talked about my stealthy exit; it seemed to happen spontaneously, as if she too knew we would be in trouble if caught. We never talked about what happened those nights in the pool; the acts somehow belonged to the dark silence of the water.

Afterward Steve and I would whisper from our open bedroom windows across the driveway that separated our parents' houses, planning the next day's events and ending with "I like you best. Good night." We were best friends, but there was something more—we had an attachment that I didn't have the words to express or even understand at the time. We lived in a small town in Pennsylvania. It was the late 1970s, and we had only heard the word "lesbian" used in reference to ugly women who wanted men and women to share the same public toilet. We heard the word in connection with "feminist" and with the whispered insults of "man haters" and "child molesters." No one talked about sex, love, lust, or masturbation. I felt like the only girl in the world whose nipples were erect, whose clit tingled, and whose cunt got wet. And if I was the only one who felt this way, what did it matter that I felt this way because of another girl? Hanging over me, however, was the overwhelming sensation that something was wicked about my feelings. Somehow in all that sexual silence I understood that if I expressed my feelings for Steve, walls would tumble in on me, exposing me as a freak, a pervert(a lesbian child molester.

Steve found a girl-on-girl porno magazine in her parents' room, tucked between the mattress and box spring. The pages were well-handled and the binding was bent over. Locked in my bedroom, she showed me the pictures of fluffy women with long red nails, shaved mounds, and larger-than-life breasts. Sitting on my canopy bed in silence, we slowly turned the pages and examined the pictures. We were thirteen. When we were done she stood up, plunging her hands deep into her jean pockets. Her eyes fixed in front of me on some mysterious invisible spot on the pink carpet; she stumbled over the words like they were Latin: "I was wondering, well, if...we can ever try that?"

Thrilled and terrified by what I was being handed, and flattered by her innocence in a desire I thought only I felt, I said, "Yes."

She didn't move or look up at me. Half afraid she had changed her mind, and half certain she had not, I stood in front of her, placing one hand on either side of her face. I turned her head up so her eyes were level with mine. "I said yes," I repeated.

I let my hands drop to my side and lay across the bed on my back, spreading my legs slightly, like I had seen women in movies do. After a few seconds that seemed like an eternity, Steve carefully climbed on top of me.

Uncertain what the tingling between my legs was really about, the weight of her body on top of me and the smell of her adolescent sweat made me wet. I let her kiss me. First, soft closemouthed kisses like aunts give; then openmouthed kisses that let our tongues explore; then long hard extended kisses where the flesh of our lips seemed to bond and our hips moved against each other's pubic bones in clumsy semi-rhythmic movement. I stopped her when her hand slipped under my light summer T-shirt. That was all.

For weeks, we danced. Each day she explored more of me, except for days when I stopped her where I had the day before. I never went any further on her body than I allowed her to go on mine, even though she never stopped me. We always started at the beginning, with kisses that I made her initiate. The thrill of exploring a body that was not mine and the excitement of her hands on my body were the only things I could think about. We silently arranged to spend more time alone together. Everything we did was new, perfect, and done for the very first time ever in the history of womankind.

One day, after a month of slow exploration, Steve slipped

one of her fingers inside my cunt as we lay naked on my floor. She probed around, moving her finger in and out of my opening. She pulled wetness out and spread it on my clit and labia. I did the same to her. Then she moved her body down, putting her mouth on my cunt. I put my hand on her head and said no. She didn't stop. She licked my fleshy folds, stuck her tongue and fingers inside of me, and licked my clit in an imitation of the pictures we had.

"No," I repeated over and over, clasping my fingers in her hair. "No, no, no." But I meant yes, and if she had stopped, I would have been furious. I felt consumed by her desire to have me in her mouth, her outright refusal to stop, and our innocent passion. On my back, with her face between my legs, I felt both helpless and more powerful than I had felt in my life. Her desire to consume my body, to please me, was stronger than her willingness to obey me. Steve made me come that afternoon, the first time I had come with anyone but myself, and I made her come with my fingers the next day. After that, she never had to ask, and I never stopped her. We rushed through the kissing, the touching of breasts, and the sucking of nipples to get to our pussies. Eventually, we both became more obsessed with exploring my body than hers. She spent the summer, fall, and part of winter fucking me in my bedroom, her bedroom, the shed, the field, the neighbor's tree house, under my family's pool deck, under her family's pool deck, and in the dark cool wine cellar in my basement.

figuring it out

stefka

I hated cheerleaders. Actually, I hated just about everybody in high school, but cheerleaders were at the top of my list. They were so perky, happy, and secretly devious, and every chance they got, they singled me out for ridicule. I was such an oddball that even my sister denied my existence every chance she had. To add to my misery, I was secretly enamored of one cheerleader in particular. I couldn't understand why I felt the way I did, but every time she was near me I got hot, I started to sweat, and I couldn't breathe right. It didn't make any sense to me.

Her name was Heather, and she was a blond goddess with a killer smile, a sunny attitude, and a body to match. She sat right in front of me in English, and staring at her long blond hair, not to mention inhaling her fresh scent every day, was pure torture. To add to my confusion, my fingers itched to bury themselves in her golden locks and I didn't know why. To make matters even worse, every time she turned to hand me papers or ask a question, my usually sharp and witty tongue knotted itself, leaving me to grunt and blush as she smiled at me.

The '80s were a time for nonconformity and pastel colors. With the girls trying to be Pat Benatar look-alikes, and their jock boyfriends wearing pink, I didn't fit in with my choice of simple jeans and sweatshirts. My short hair was hidden under a ball cap, while all the other girls sported feathered bangs or wings. I couldn't blend in if I tried. Despite this, Heather tried to engage me in conversation every chance she got, and my silly brain, weird body, and rebellious tongue wouldn't let me tell her to shove off. Instead, I gaped at her, my face flaming and my heart pounding as my mouth grunted every response. I was a dork in a major way, yet she seemed to genuinely like me.

My misery was compounded by the fact that I needed a math tutor. For all my brilliance, I couldn't pass a simple math class. When I found out Heather would tutor me, I wanted to crawl in a hole and pray for Armageddon and jump for joy at the same time. I was screwed.

My anguish and delight continued to grow as we spent more and more time together. Her friends poked fun at me, and she often came to my defense, putting an arm around my shoulders. Her warm touch sent shivers of joy through my body, conflicting with my innate hatred for cheerleaders. It bothered me, and I hated and loved her even more. I couldn't stand to be near her, but I ached when I wasn't. Something had to give soon.

Graduation was fast approaching, and the pressure to pass math increased, as did my feelings for her. I didn't know whether I should scream or kiss her. Both of us were due to head to different colleges, and I knew the moment summer hit I would no longer have to deal with whatever was happening to me. This both depressed and relieved me.

Everything came crashing down one night when I went to her house for tutoring. My final math test loomed, and Heather felt I needed extra help, so she told me to come over on a Saturday. When I arrived, she informed me that her parents and brother were gone, not due to return home until Sunday. That made me nervous, because until that point, someone had always been with us. For the first hour and a half I kept my nerves under wraps and tried to focus on the problems, but with her being so close, fighting the urge to touch her was killing me. I found myself focusing on how she breathed rather than on this train traveling from one place to the next while another train traveled in the opposite direction.

She wore shorts and a short-sleeve shirt, as did I, because Southern California weather, as usual, was rather warm. The brush of her thighs against mine drove me to distraction. I tried to ignore it, but after a while it was all I thought about. Her skin was soft, with a hint of gold from the sun. Her fresh scent invaded my senses, until polynomials and parameters faded from my head. Instead of trying to figure out the degrees of a triangle, I tried to calculate how many degrees my body temperature rose with each passing minute. Pretty soon, I was befuddled by my body's reactions, and everything I had learned vacated the premises. She became the center of my attention.

Finally, I couldn't take it anymore. Two hours of enduring her touch, trying to concentrate on math, and wondering why she was being so nice to me had taken its toll. I slammed my book closed, tossed my pencil onto the table, and ran my hands through my hair. I had to get out of there. I had started to gather my things when she placed her warm hand on my arm.

I looked at the hand like it was a live wire, because it sent searing shocks through my body. I couldn't meet her eyes, because I was afraid she would see how I felt about her. Her hand disappeared, only to return with the other one, cupping my flushed face, turning it toward hers.

Her blue eyes were dark as they searched my face. I couldn't look away. I was a fly caught in a web. For what seemed like an eternity we stared at each other. Then, without a word, her lips touched mine. I jerked in surprise but didn't move away. After a few seconds, she pulled back slightly, her own lips wet. I was too stunned to say anything, but something must have shown on my face, because she smiled broadly before swooping down for another kiss.

My body's reaction was astounding. I was on fire. She certainly knew what she was doing, but I had never kissed anyone, let alone another girl. My sanity left me, and all I could do was kiss back. In that moment, in that kiss, I let everything I had ever felt for her pour through me, into her. I felt her guiding me onto the couch and I let her; it felt so right kissing her. For the first time, I felt right about everything. Her lips never left my face as one of her hands traveled slowly down my shirt and lifted it. The brush of her fingers against my stomach made me jump, sparking more fire between my legs. I must have whimpered or sighed, because her chest rumbled and her knee slipped between mine, pressing hard against me.

I was molten lava, and I melted against her knee, rocking gently. I had no idea what I was doing; I just copied whatever she did to me. When her hand pressed against my breasts, I did the same to her. We were mirrors. I thought of nothing but her. Every touch added to the fire between my legs. I heard whimpers and sighs but didn't know if they were hers or mine. When her lips finally left mine to taste my nipple, I arched and moaned. I couldn't believe it was happening. All my dreams, those tormenting dreams, were nothing compared to the real thing. I wanted to scream, but this time in ecstasy.

Time stood still as she explored my body, and when she finally reached the burning pit at my very center, I was on edge. My heart pounded and I couldn't think coherently. All I wanted was to fall off the cliff; all I needed was a push. When her questing fingers touched my clit, I fell.

My knee jammed against her moist shorts, and as I jerked she rocked harder against my knee until we both stiffened and sighed. I didn't know what had happened, but my body felt like a wet noodle and I couldn't move a muscle. We lay pressed against each other on the couch, breathing heavily while I tried to sort out what had happened. All I knew was that I liked what she had done, and I wanted to do it again… but this time I wanted to touch her.

Somehow I found the strength to shift just enough to reach her shorts. Her face still pressed against my neck, I began kissing her as my trembling hand slipped inside the elastic band and touched the smooth skin there. She jerked but didn't move away, which encouraged me to continue. Her moist pussy greeted my fingers, and without knowing how I knew what to do, I slipped one finger inside her and received a breathy sigh in return. Pleased, I began to move my finger in and out in the small amount of space I had, and she began to quiver and press against it. Her breathing picked up rapidly as I brushed my thumb against her hard clit.

Her reaction spurred me on, and I quickly moved my finger and thumb to the rhythm of her hips until she arched against me and gasped. Her thighs clamped around my hand as she rode it, and I smiled. After a few minutes of rest, she wrestled me to the ground and pinned me. Somehow she managed to get my shorts completely off before maneuvering herself between my legs. She did things with her tongue I had no names for. She gave me no time to think as her tongue licked and teased me in places I didn't know existed. My body shook with pleasure as she continually licked and stroked me with her hands.

My first taste of her was another shock to my system. She was so sweet tasting, I couldn't get enough. She never gave me a break to catch my breath, as if she didn't want me to think about anything but what was happening. Even when we made it to her room, I didn't think of anything but her. I was happy, and I didn't want to spoil it. We took turns like that all night, the two of us learning each other's bodies and what we wanted. We hardly spoke, whispering only short sentences and breathy words of encouragement. We slept that night wrapped in each other's arms.

It wasn't until I got home the next day that my thoughts returned to normal. Reality finally hit me. I was insane. How could I have thought that what had occurred between Heather and I was right? We were two girls, and as far as I knew that was highly frowned upon. As I pursued that train of thought, more insane ideas crept in. Was what we had done part of an elaborate joke between her and her friends? To show how much of a freak I really was? But if that was the case, why had Heather appeared to enjoy it? Maybe she was a good actress. Nothing made sense. But one thing I did know, I could not let it happen again. I was already a freak, but if I did that with Heather again, I would become even more of a freak.

From then on, I never spoke to her. I ignored her, moved my seat, and refused to take her calls. By the time graduation hit, I had thoroughly achieved my goals: I had passed math, and Heather hated me. When I walked down the aisle to receive my diploma, I saw her crushed and angry face. I may have succeeded in passing math, but my greatest accomplishment was ruining the best thing that had ever happened to me.

I didn't see her again until nearly two years later. I was in the college cafeteria getting my lunch when a woman came up to me and spoke my name. I didn't recognize her until she was close, and when I did, I was stunned. Gone was the golden mane, and in its place was short, spiky hair tipped with black. Instead of her pastel sweaters and chinos she wore ripped, faded jeans with a white tank top and leather jacket. When I had known her she had only two earrings in her ears, but now she had at least ten in one and five in the other. Heather had rarely worn makeup, but this new gal liked the color black, and her gorgeous blue eyes were surrounded by it.

She was still the stunning goddess I had known, yet it seemed she had let the rebel inside take over. It was a pleasant surprise. I too had changed. Gone were the ball caps, jeans, and sweatshirts. In their place were ruffled blouses, styled hair, and skirts. I had exchanged my backpack for a briefcase and sneakers for boots. She followed me to a table, and for a few minutes we talked about nothing, then she cocked her head and gave me a look.

"So, have you figured it out?" she asked, as she reached out and touched my hand.

"Figured what out?" I asked, confused.

She gave me a wicked smile, pulled my notebook closer to her, took a black marker from her jacket pocket, and scribbled her number before standing up.

"Give me a call when you do. Then we can continue what we started two years ago."

Still puzzled, I looked up at her. Her smile grew. She bent down and captured my lips with hers in a long, hard kiss before she turned around and sauntered off. I touched my lips in confusion and watched her go.

Twenty years have passed since then, and there isn't a day that goes by when I don't wish I'd saved her number, to tell her thanks if nothing else. A year later, I finally did figure things out, and if it hadn't been for Heather, I probably never would have.

pussy, american-style

●

heather towne

My first year of college was pretty dull. I got good grades, but living at home with my parents, I never felt I was getting the full university experience. So, at the start of my second year I moved into a dorm room and, man, did I get a true taste of campus life, among other things.

Two girls lived in each dorm room, and since I didn't know anyone well enough to ask to be my roommate, the college matched me up with a foreign student—Isabelle, a girl from Spain. She didn't know a lot of English, and I knew even less Spanish, but she had a warm personality, and since her parents were paying a humongous tuition fee, she was dedicated to making the most of her American education before returning to Barcelona.

And after only a couple of weeks together, Isabelle and I had become fast friends. She was an extremely intelligent girl, with a shy but wicked sense of humor and a passion for the arts that matched mine. She liked a lot of the same authors and musicians I did, and enjoyed a good time too, like I did.

I invited her to my parents' house for the weekend. They were away at a medical conference, so us girls had the run of the big old house. We took full advantage, doing things that certainly would have yielded a hall warning back home at the dorm—like throwing a party with some classmates that lasted into the wee hours, playing our tunes megaloud, drinking, and smoking. And it was early that Sunday morning, when the last of the revelers from our all-nighter had finally left, that Isabelle and I—buzzed and alone together—got to know each other more intimately than I had ever thought possible.

I decided to take a shower before hitting the hay, using the soothing spray to dampen my high spirits. I was letting the hot water soak into my tingling body when I heard the bathroom door open. I peeked around the shower curtain and spied Isabelle tiptoeing into the room. "Hi, girl!" I greeted her eagerly.

She almost jumped out of her golden-brown skin, then stared as I grinned at her. "Sorry, Lisa," she said, once she got her breath back. "I just get some water." She held up a glass.

"No problemo, Belle," I said. "I was done anyway." I turned off the jet of water and stepped out of the huge freestanding bathtub, my body shimmering. "Hand me a towel, will you."

She set her glass on the counter and pulled a thick towel off the rack. But instead of handing it to me, she stood there, staring unabashedly at my pussy.

I laughed. "Never seen a cunny before?"

She lifted her big brown eyes up to my face, then sent them flying back down to my pussy. "Yes," she said, oddly solemn. "I mean no… I mean, never one so…bare."

"Huh? Oh, yeah, I shave it once a week. Lots of American girls do."

"Why?"

"Uh, well, some people think it looks better that way. And it increases the pleasure of, you know, sex."

She continued to examine my pussy, long enough to make me blush and feel just a little nervous. "I see," she said finally,

adding another tidbit of knowledge to her New World education. She reracked the towel, looked me in the eye, and asked,
"You show me how?"

I was taken aback, and while I was wasting my time thinking about her unusual request, she stripped off her silk paja-
mas and got as naked as I was. Her body was stunning! Her
breasts were high and firm, medium size, with thick, dark
nipples. Her stomach was flat, her waist narrow, her legs long,
smooth, and toned. And the area between her legs was covered with the thickest thatch of black fur I'd ever seen on a
pussy—assuming there *was* a pussy buried underneath all
that pubic hair.

"You shave me," she stated, her eyes sparkling as her even
white teeth flashed a smile. She ran her fingers through her
long, shiny black hair, letting it cascade down her back.

I gulped, the humid air suddenly growing thicker and
steamier. "I—I guess I could show you...how to do it..." I
stammered.

She opened the medicine cabinet, looked around inside for
a moment, then plucked out one of my mom's disposable
razors and a can of my dad's shaving cream. "No. You shave
me," she repeated, pointing back and forth between the two of
us. She smiled a wicked grin that left me weak in the knees. "I
learn more quick that way."

So, helped along by the copious quantities of alcohol I'd
consumed, and further fired up by the sight of Isabelle's lush,
bronze body, I shed my inhibitions, and the Spanish girl and I
ended up in the antique tub together. She lay back in the warm
water, fully submerging her gorgeous body, except for her pert
tits and chocolate nipples, which peeped above the waterline,
while I sat in front of her wielding the razor and can of shaving cream.

"Shall we begin?" I asked, smiling uncertainly as I marveled
at the girl's breathtaking beauty.

"Yes, begin," she replied, sliding forward and wrapping her supple legs around my waist, basically dropping her pussy in my lap.

I swallowed hard, telling myself I owed it to this Euro überbabe to impart whatever wisdom I possessed, while my damp-with-other-than-water pussy urged me to just fucking hurry up. I sprayed some shaving cream into my shaking hand and tentatively foamed her up. She quickly reached out and put her hand over mine, helping me rub the cool lubricant all around and over her pussy, moaning slightly as my fingers inadvertently-on-purpose touched her clit.

She locked her glittering eyes onto mine as we sensuously prepped her pussy for defoliation. "You are good-looking girl, Lisa," she whispered.

The passionate contessa was turned on big-time, and so was I. There was no turning back now. "Thanks. You too," I mumbled, as her eyes traveled down my body until they rested on my big, milky white boobs and pink, painfully erect nipples. "I, um…think you're about lathered up good enough now."

"Shave me, then," Isabelle hissed. "Shave my cunny, Heather."

I nodded, rinsed my hands, and picked up the razor off the edge of the tub. I let the plastic beauty aid dangle just above her whitened bush for a minute, trembling slightly, then tightened my grip and started stroking.

"Yes," she murmured, closing her eyes and grasping her glistening tits in her little brown hands. She squeezed and fondled her damp mounds.

I tried to concentrate on what I was doing—shaving a gorgeous girl's pussy while she played with her luscious boobs. It was almost too much for my shattered senses to handle, but I managed, barely, to bring myself under control and slide the razor through the foam and the fur above her cunt. I gently trimmed away the hair on her lower body, until the razor quickly became clogged and I had to fumble with the taps behind me, starting a warm stream of water to rinse the razor.

Isabelle rubbed the area of bare flesh I had left behind and said, "Feels good."

I told her to spread her legs even wider, and then really went to work skimming away her bush. I shaved the remaining pubes above her pussy, sliding the razor up and down and rinsing it out until she showed skin from belly button to clitty. Then I sucked some more air into my billowing lungs, held my tongue between my teeth, and slowly shaved around the left side of her delicate lips.

"Yes," she moaned, her body twitching every time I passed the blade over her sensitive flesh, stroking her hot pussy lips with cold steel. She grabbed her left breast and squeezed, rolling her engorged nipple between her fingers, her nails flashing silver, and then slid her right hand over her wet belly until her fingers rested on her clit.

It was a difficult enough procedure, shaving another girl's pussy, without that sexy babe getting herself off at the same time. I was coated with perspiration, and the heavy, humid air was almost impossible to breathe, but I somehow managed to finish shaving the left side of her pussy and moved over to the right.

"God, it feels so good, Lisa," she whimpered, rubbing her raw, naked lips.

"Looks good, too," I said in a quavery voice. I set about clearing away the rest of her hair-down-there, desperately trying to ignore my own boiling desire. And with three more deft strokes of the blade, I had the Spanish hottie as bare as any American porn princess.

"All done," I blurted, relieved that I hadn't nicked the sweet young thing in the most private of all girlish places. I splashed water on her beautifully bald pussy as she continued fingering herself.

"Thank you, thank you," she breathed, her fingers moving faster and faster, until they were almost a blur.

"Thank *you*," I said, boldly shoving two fingers into her cunt and pumping. It was time to really get to know her pussy—the feel and the taste of it.

"Yes, Lisa!" she cried. "You fuck me!"

She was incredibly wet and hot and tight. I slid my purple-tipped digits back and forth inside her brazenly bare pussy, as she frantically buffed her swollen clit. Faster and faster I pounded her with my fingers, and faster and faster she burnished her nub, until she screamed out with unrepentant joy and her beautiful body jerked with orgasm. Her boobs jounced up and down as she jolted with ecstasy. She came over and over, her fingers on her clit and her tit, my fingers buried inside her pussy.

"That's the way, baby! Come for me, Isabelle!" I yelled, figer-fucking her in a frenzy, sweat streaming off my face and onto her heaving, shining torso.

When she had calmed down at last, I pulled out my dripping fingers and licked off her come. She smiled weakly up at me, licked her red, puffy lips, and said, "Now I pleasure you."

We reversed positions in the slippery tub, and she got me to drape my long legs over either side of the bath so she could clutch my butt cheeks and bring my burning snatch up to her mouth. "You taste good," she murmured, lapping at my sopping pussy in long, slow tongue strokes, all the way from my asshole to my clit.

"Eat me," was all I could mutter as I clung to the sides of the tub and watched the hot-blooded honey lick my slit. My pussy tingled with each and every tongue lash, and a heavy heat rose up from my cunny and engulfed my body.

She lapped and lapped at my pussy with her thick, pink tongue, hungrily feeding on my cunt. She teased my electrified clit with her flicking tongue tip, and then took the swollen nub between her lips and sucked on it.

"Omigod!" I cried, my head dizzy, my body on fire. "I'm going to come!"

Isabelle kept right on sucking my clit, kneading my buns, and tugging on my rosy-red bud until a tremendous orgasm welled up from the spot where her mouth met my cunt and I was blistered by ecstasy. My body quivered with erotic shock as an orgasm tore me apart. I held on to the sides of the tub for dear life, my brain and body reeling, as Isabelle licked up and swallowed my hot, gushing girl juices.

My orgasm felt like an eternity. In real life, it was probably no more than a minute. I collapsed into the bottom of the bath, the searing sexual aftershocks subsiding only slowly. Isabelle leaned over me and kissed me softly on the lips, then let me nibble exhaustedly on her dark, rubbery nips and paw at her breasts. "You have good time? You learn something?" she asked.

"Both," I gasped in reply.

That same day, Isabelle and I awoke in each other's arms and were rapidly reenergized by the amazing realization of what we had done only eight hours earlier; we stiff-legged it back into the bathroom and picked up our shaving sex right where we had left off.

"This time, I shave you," Isabelle said excitedly, picking up a new razor and the can of shaving cream. "Practice makes perfect, no?"

I pretended to look thoughtful for a moment. "Well...I normally shave on Monday...but I guess I can make an exception if it'll further your education."

She giggled and playfully slapped my bare bottom.

We stepped back into the tub, drew the shower curtain all the way around the steamy sex spot, and turned on the water from the shower nozzle this time. We pranced around under the stinging needle-points for a bit, getting ourselves all wet and hot and bothered, and then I grabbed Isabelle in my arms and kissed her.

"Mmm," she breathed into my mouth.

We kissed long and hard, the water dancing over our gloriously naked bodies. I held her slippery figure tight in my arms, jamming our tits and nipples together, and then I let my hands loose to wander all over her lightly muscled back, down to her big, bold ass. I cupped her fleshy cheeks and squeezed them. She moaned, and I swallowed her cries of pleasure. Then I parted her full lips with my hardened pink spear and jammed my tongue toward her tongue. We Frenched ferociously, our tongues swirling together over and over, gleefully slapping against each other in girlish delight and devilish passion.

She pulled her head back and said, "It is time you...come clean." She briefly licked my lips and then broke our embrace to bend down and pick up the shaving utensils—or, as far as I was concerned, sex toys.

She instructed me to lift my arms up over my head, and then she moved me forward, out of the stream of heated water, and lathered up my armpits. The dense foam felt wonderfully cool on my vulnerable underarms. I interlaced my fingers and lolled my head back as she applied the sexual primer.

"Don't move," she cautioned. She squirted more shaving cream into her hand and rubbed it on my legs, all over my legs, till my slender limbs were covered in white film from thigh to ankle. "Almost done," she said, as she fired a final dollop of cream at my pussy and rubbed between my legs.

I trembled with excitement as I anxiously anticipated the raw, red-hot sensation that I knew the stroking razor would elicit. I didn't have to wait long. Isabelle stood up, squeezed my supersensitive tits with one hand while she gripped the razor with the other, and began shaving me under my arms. She shaved one tender, ticklish armpit in slow, delicious strokes, and then the other, stopping every now and then to suck on my blossomed nipples and tongue my boobs.

She dropped to her knees and started shaving my legs. I watched her with feverish eyes, cupping my breasts and pinching my nipples, my legs quivering as she trimmed them of what little hair they had. And in all too quick a time, she had shaved my legs smooth and gone to work on my pussy.

"I must be careful here," she said, looking up at me, her eyes shining.

"Just shave it, baby," I groaned, wild with want.

She gripped my ass and brought the razor to bear on my very short curlies. She stroked around my throbbing clit and puffy lips, taking it slow and steady. It was immensely erotic, her face a pretty mask of concentration.

"Now I check my work," she stated when she had finished shaving my cunt of its thin blonde coating. She got to her feet and directed the steamy rush of water over my burning body, cleaning away all the remaining suds. Then she pushed my arms back up and inspected my armpits with her fingers.

I giggled at first, then started groaning when she replaced her fingers with her tongue and the erotic charge hit me full-force. She lapped at my bare pits, her wet tongue tracing fire all over those two most vulnerable spots. I'd never felt anything like it; it was stunningly intimate and sexual. She licked and licked each armpit in turn, then squatted and ran her amazing tongue along the insides of my thighs as the hot water cascaded over my flaming body.

"Tongue my cunny, Isabelle!" I urged as I grabbed hold of her damp, shiny hair and tried to pull her head closer to my smoldering pussy.

She licked and gently bit the delicate skin of my inner thighs, and then, finally, brought her wonderfully wicked tongue into my cunt. She used her pleasure tool to part my swollen lips, probing my cunny with her tongue. My legs buckled as she spread my pussy lips with her hand and buffed my aching clit with her thumb, all the time driving my cunt with her tongue.

"Fuck, yeah!" I screamed as the sexy foreigner tongue-fucked my pussy and rubbed my clitty. I came over and over, ravaged by orgasms like never before, the shaving foreplay having honed my overwrought senses to razor-thin sharpness.

Twice a week now, Isabelle and I give each other a full-body shave. And we don't confine our sensual grooming habits to the privacy of our own, or my parents', bathroom either. We've trimmed each other in the women's shower room in the university athletic center, in the sauna at the local Y, and even on a deserted, night-shaded beach. The only constant is that our stubble-humper sessions always end in awesome mutual orgasms. We're even considering shaving our heads, but we might save that special treat for our summer vacation.

wwbd: what would brett do?

●

therese szymanski

I write a sleazy lesbian mystery series featuring a charac-
ter named Brett. She's a big, bad butch who always gets the
girl, and I sometimes think her persona takes me over.
Somehow, though, I think Brett would be able to get the
two beautiful, young women in this story completely
naked and all the way to Happy-land without having her
eyebrows tweezed first.

One evening, my girlfriend and I were bringing in my groceries when the door across from mine opened.

"Oh," a cute blond said, looking at us. "I thought someone
was knocking on my door."

"Nope. Just us. I'm Reese. I live here." I stuck my paw out.

She shook it. "I'm Nancy. I just moved in." Her hand was soft.

I looked over her shoulder and saw furniture pieces strewn
everywhere. "Um, I have tools, so if you need anything, just let
me know."

"Oh, thank you! We've been trying to put this armoire
together all week!"

I'd offered tools, not labor, but it appeared I was now backed into a corner. Great. I'd planned to spend the night working on the next book in my mystery series about Brett Higgins, butch extraordinaire. "Uh, yeah. OK. Fine. We just need to bring this stuff in, and I'll be right over."

After putting away the groceries, my girl took off for her own place, and I, relegated to my fate, went across the hall with my toolbox.

"Oh, thank God!" Nancy said, opening the door. "You're good at this sort of stuff?"

"Yeah, I am." Pressboard parts covered the floor. I picked up the instructions and started work.

"Yo, dude," a young woman said, entering, carrying a twelve-pack of Bud Light and a pizza.

"Oh, Liza, this is Reese. She lives across the hall. She's helping put this stuff together. Reese, this is Liza. She's staying with me while she's wait-listed for her own apartment."

"We both just got transferred out here," Liza explained. She appeared a bit older than Nancy—old enough to buy beer, at least.

"Hey, Reese," Nancy said. "You want pizza? Beer?"

"Uh, no thanks. I'm good." For the next two hours, I worked and they kept me company. Liza was twenty-one, and Nancy was eighteen. They were friends from back home in California. They used to be cheerleaders, but not together, because they didn't go to the same high school. Liza had a boyfriend who was in the slammer, and Nancy's fiancé would join her soon.

Liza was a bold, brash, tattooed brunet. She quickly clued in to me being a big ol' dyke, but we almost had to draw diagrams for the naïve Nancy. Before long, I realized I needed all my tools, so I fetched my drill and ratchets, glad to have tools for all occasions. I also brought my own beer because I don't like Bud.

We all drank and talked while I screwed and hammered.

"We just have to wait for the glue to dry, and we can put the drawers in." Liza helped me push the armoire upright.

"Ooh," Nancy said, "do you think maybe—"

"She wants to know if you can help us with the entertainment center," Liza translated, pointing at another box in a corner.

"I understand if you need to get going," Nancy said. "I mean, you've already helped us *so* much. But…"

"We really spent, like, the entire week trying to put this thing together," Liza said.

"Oh, what the hell. I can't overlook damsels in distress. Let me just get some more beer."

"Ooh, can we see your place?" Nancy asked.

I wished I had cleaned yesterday, like I'd planned. But I shrugged and said, "Sure." I led them to my place. "Kitchen. Living room. Dining room."

"Wow, dude, ya like this writer or what?" Liza said, noticing my shelf of author's copies.

I grinned at her and pulled one off the shelf, showing her my picture on the back cover. "I *am* the writer."

"Omigod, you write books!" Nancy said. They both seemed kinda buzzed, and Lord knew I should probably not be driving, operating heavy machinery, or even using power tools. What can I say? I'm *B.A.D.*

I shrugged. "Just a few. I'm mostly a copywriter." I led them to the back of the apartment. "Here's the bathroom and the bedroom. Not much, but it's mine."

"Um, what's that?" Nancy asked, pointing at my toy shelves.

Thank God I'd been drinking! But I still blushed. "Toys."

"Sex toys?"

"Uh, yeah."

"I've never…" Nancy said. "Can you show them to us? Please?"

"This is hot," Liza said, sitting on my bed to read something from *When the Dancing Stops*, my first Brett mystery.

"What is?" Nancy asked, flushing as Liza showed her a passage. "That's not…possible? Is it?" Nancy looked up. "Is it?"

All the sex I write is based on personal experience, so I knew whatever Nancy had read was possible. I suspected the young straight girl had come across a fisting scene. "Yeah, it's possible." I grinned.

"So, are you going to show us your toys?"

"Yeah," Liza said. "I'm curious."

"Oh, for fuck's sake," I said. "Whatever." I started pulling out lubes and nipple clamps. Dental dams, condoms, and butt plugs, *oh my*. Wide-eyed, Nancy absorbed my explanations while Liza looked as if she knew it all.

Nancy's mind was boggled, especially after I explained that because women give birth to babies, they really can take *that* size dildo—and in fact, one of my het female friends had referred to my largest as "Hung like a horse," and she'd meant it in a good way.

"I've never even kissed a woman," Nancy said when we got back to her apartment. I set about realigning the drawers in her armoire. Rising, I took a sip of my sixth beer, and looked at the two of them standing side by side.

Nancy teased Liza. "You won't say you *haven't* done it with a woman. Or women." Nancy looked at me. "And you—you're all gay and stuff, and I've never even kissed a woman." She seductively licked her lips.

I looked at them. Now, I love kissing, and a first kiss can really be something to write about. But, upsettingly, common sense chose that moment to introduce itself—I was drunk, they were drunk, we were neighbors. Things could go horribly wrong if I tried to remedy Nancy's lack of knowledge. "Um, well, you two have at it then. Feel free to play." If I couldn't play, then a front-row seat for two girls going at it was almost as good. "Have at. I'm not stopping you." *Down, Brett, down!*

Liza cupped Nancy's face and drew it near her own, then leaned down and touched her lips to her friend's. Their lips slowly caressed each other's, and Liza's pink-tipped tongue entered Nancy's mouth.

Blond Nancy, brunet Liza. Young. Nice bodies. Long hair. Hot women. Kissing. Slowly starting to touch…exploring each other's body with light caresses… I was mesmerized.

They pulled apart, still looking at each other. Nancy slid her hands up her own body, cupping her breasts and squeezing her nipples. Liza put her hands over Nancy's, helping her.

"I want to see both of you," Nancy said, pulling off her shirt and bra. "C'mon," she said to Liza, then me. "You wear a sports bra, don't you?" she asked, pressing herself against me and wrapping her arms around my neck.

I pushed her hands from my breasts. I thought of those bracelets and ball caps some Christians wear, the ones with WWJD for "What Would Jesus Do?" Well, I knew what Brett would do!

I pulled Nancy against me, letting her ride my thigh, then ran my hands over her half-naked body, enjoying her soft skin. I fondled her breasts and squeezed her nipples, and she raised her fingers to my face, running the tips over my eyebrows.

"I bet you could be really pretty if you wanted," Nancy said. "How about we give you a makeover?"

"Uh, don't hold your breath, 'kay, babe?"

"Nancy, you did get the entire 'she's butch' bit, right?" Liza said, walking behind her and wrapping an arm around her waist.

"You've both seen me, now I want to see you," Nancy said. "Take off your shirts." She focused on Liza, wrapping her arms around her and kissing her again. Leisurely, Liza fondled Nancy's breasts. Again.

God, I wanted these fine young women!

Nancy tugged Liza's midriff-baring wife-beater, pulling it over her head. She had problems with Liza's bra, though, so I undid it with a snap of my fingers.

"God, that feels nice," Nancy said about my hands on her breasts. "We'll both get naked if you'll let me put makeup on you," she said as she hesitantly fondled Liza's breasts.

"Whoa," Liza said. "You can't be makin' no promises for me." She nibbled Nancy's neck.

I pinched Nancy' nipples. She squirmed, putting her hands over mine in encouragement. Slowly, she lowered the zipper on her tight jeans. "You want me to take these off?"

I looked over her shoulder at Liza, who smirked. "Take 'em off, Nancy," she said. "Then we'll give little Reese here a makeover. I think her eyebrows could use some plucking."

I grabbed Liza, pushing her against the wall. I leaned down and sucked a nipple between my teeth. My hand slipped down to her zipper.

Liza put her hand over mine. "Nuh uh, stud. You want these offa me, you let Nancy have her wicked little way with you."

I cupped Liza's ass while I sucked her other nipple. Then I felt warmness spread across my back, and I reached behind me to caress Nancy's naked shin. I glanced up to see them kissing again.

I took Liza's zipper in my teeth, but again she blocked my move. "Nancy, get your tweezers."

So, that's how I ended up sitting on my neighbor's radiator while she plucked my eyebrows and applied base, blush, mascara, and lipstick. Meanwhile, I ran my hands over her soft hips, caressed the insides of her thighs, then pulled her down so I could kiss her soft lips, running my tongue across them and slowly sliding into the warmth of her mouth.

Liza leaned back, watching us. She ran her tongue over her

full lips, popped the button on her jeans, then pulled down the zipper. Have you ever noticed just how erotic the sound of a lowering zip is?

Nancy leaned against me and said, "I want to see you…show me…what you wrote about. With Liza."

"Oh, with Liza, eh?" I said. "Not you?"

Nancy flushed.

I glanced at Liza, nodding at her jeans. She grinned, making sure I watched as she exposed her long, trim legs and neatly shaven cunt.

I wrapped my arm around Nancy, dipping my head to engage her lips again. Reaching down, I trailed my fingers through her wetness. I lowered her to the ground. Liza lay next to us, smirking as she played her fingertips over Nancy's collarbone, down her breast, and over her stomach, eventually joining mine between Nancy's legs.

"Oh, God," Nancy said, writhing as we entered her simultaneously.

I kissed down her body, taking a moment to suckle her breasts, teasing her nipples with my teeth, and nibbling slightly, before lying between her legs and blowing against her wetness. Liza removed her fingers to toy with Nancy's breasts, but I moved into the void, curling two fingers inside Nancy as I licked her up and down.

"Oh, God," Nancy said, wriggling. "Oh, God…nobody's ever…oh, yes…" She spread her legs as wide as she could, bucking up into my face.

I got the message. I had started slowly, running my tongue up and down her while Liza kissed her, took care of her breasts, and nibbled at her neck. Now I sped up, sucking her clit, beating it back and forth with my tongue while I fingerfucked her, in and out, pushing hard and fast, rubbing her G spot with each thrust.

"Yes, please!" Nancy screamed, clamping her legs around

my shoulders. I quickly pulled my right arm up, since I'd previously dislocated that shoulder twice during sex. Nancy rode my face and hand, her thighs holding me as she tried to whip me about—but I held her in place.

"Oh, fuck me!"

I pulled the orgasm out of her, making it last until she sobbed for air. Then, I climbed up her body and kissed her deeply.

When we separated, Liza lay next to us, smirking.

"Now, I want to see you do Liza," Nancy said. "Like you wrote in that book."

I looked over her naked body, at the other woman. "Then I'm gonna need some lube."

"I'll get it," Nancy said, jumping to her feet and grabbing my keys from my toolbox, not bothering to get dressed.

"You're such a tease," I said to Liza, who lay nonchalantly on her side, her legs demurely crossed.

She grinned, reached up, and ran her thumb over my lower lip. "But that shade of lipstick is *so* you."

I grabbed her wrists and threw her on her back, pinning her arms. "You're so gonna pay for that." My legs were between hers, so I used them to spread her thighs nice and wide. I leaned down for a kiss, lightly touching my lips to hers, then running my tongue over her lips and... "Bloody bitch!" I yelled, pulling away. She'd bitten me!

She grinned, and I grabbed both her wrists with one hand. I ran my free hand over each of her breasts in turn, cupping and caressing them. Then I took a nipple between my thumb and forefinger and squeezed it, hard.

She bucked up against me. "Uh!"

I pulled, twisted, and yanked it.

"Ah, God! That hurts!"

But I knew she liked it.

"Wow!"

I looked up to see Nancy standing, naked and slack-jawed, holding my pump bottle of lube. I grabbed it, pumping single-handedly to cover my free hand. I felt between Liza's thighs, fingering her lightly. She was wet, warm, and squirming. The look on her face said she'd just realized her longtime friend was about to see her get fucked by another woman. She was gonna come for an audience.

I nibbled her neck, biting it lightly while running my fingers up and down her cunt. She was soaked. Dripping. I ran my tongue over her breasts, taking each nipple with my teeth, tugging them.

I had three fingers buried deep inside her by the time I released her wrists. I knelt between her thighs, running my left hand over her body while maintaining eye contact. I fucked her with my right hand, in and out—first one finger, then two fingers…three fingers…four.

Her eyes squeezed shut. She breathed deeply, writhing against my hand.

"Look at me," I said.

She opened her beautiful brown eyes, and we looked at each other.

"God, you're gorgeous," I said. She panted as I slid my hand into her.

"Oh, oh, God, yes," Liza said, jerking against my hand. "God, please, Reese, fuck me…"

I slid my hand out of her, curled my fingers, then rammed my entire fist back into her.

"Oh, goddamn!" Liza screamed, as her entire body jerked upward.

"Omigod," Nancy said, kneeling next to me and watching in rapt fascination.

"How's this?" I twisted my fist around inside Liza, acclimating her. She loosened around my hand.

"Yes, God, please," Liza said, moaning.

I continued to fuck her as I lay between her legs, then tasted her for the first time. "Damn, you taste good," I said. I ran my left hand over her body, wanting to remind her of her nakedness, to keep her aware of how open and exposed she was. I moved my hand up and down inside her, then I extended my fingers, stretching my hand further.

And then I fucked her with my entire hand. In and out. As I licked her up and down, I ate and fucked and fondled her, all at once.

She bucked against me, shoving her bare cunt against my face, wriggling and jiggling. "Oh, God," she said. "Fuck me—harder! Faster! Oh, fuck yeah!"

I was only aware of her and me. I pulled one nipple, squeezing it fiercely. Then I pinched the other. I sucked her clit, my tongue all over her cunt.

"Reese! Shit! Goddamn!"

Just as I thought my hand was gonna break—she was squeezing it so tightly—a flood of warm liquid poured over my wrist and onto my face.

When I pulled out, I couldn't help but wonder if this was gonna make our being neighbors awkward. I needn't have worried—things became awkward even sooner than that. Only fifteen minutes later, as I IM'ed with a friend (pretty much saying, "You just ain't gonna believe this"), I brought my hand up to my face and took a whiff. I would continue smelling her the entire next day—and I'd remember how her cunt clenched my fist for much longer than that.

Maybe I wasn't as much like Brett as some might think. After all, she'd be running after her next conquest, whereas I wanted to remember what Liza felt like. And, maybe, try to get her to have dinner with me.

But first, I really needed to run to the john and see if I had any eyebrows left.

how i ended up on my back

●

amie m. evans

Our lips are as close as they can be without touching. All our muscles are tense, tight, controlled. My lips, dark with deep burgundy lipstick, rest slightly apart. I can feel her breath on my face as she exhales. I know she can smell my lipstick and perfume as she inhales. We sit on the sofa, our bodies turned toward each other. Her hands are on my elbows. My hands are in the crooks of her bent arms; my palms rest on the slight bulge of her upper-arm muscles while my fingers wrap around the sides of her arms. I use my arms as a brace to maintain this distance between us. My arms are not a weight-bearing structure; if she applies pressure to their backs, my brace will collapse and I'll tumble into her, unable to resist her embrace.

I brush my resting lips against hers, transferring lipstick, gently teasing her mouth. I let the tip of my tongue run along the inside of her lips; her mouth opens wider, beckoning my tongue.

I plunge my tongue into her mouth, probing her as she responds to me. I close my eyes. I keep our lips from touching as long as I can. I squeeze my fingers into her arms. She pulls me toward her. Our bodies collapse against each other. She kisses me deeply, pushing her lips hard against mine; our tongues invade each other's mouths. The competing tastes of lipstick, cigarettes, scotch, and a hint of sweetness from the sugar in the soda mingle with the soft, fleshy taste of our mouths. In saliva, the flavors travel from my mouth to hers, hers to mine.

I grab the back of her head and clasp my fingers in her hair, pushing her lips harder against mine. She wraps her arm over my shoulder and around my neck. Her mouth absorbs my moan. Her other arm wraps around my waist and pulls my body harder against hers as if she is trying to assimilate my flesh. I pull away, biting her lip as I create a pocket of air between our bodies, separating us. My breath is coming in faster surges. I want her to fuck me. I know if I said, "Fuck me now," she would. I know she wants to fuck me.

I straddle her, putting one leg on either side of her lap, resting my body weight on my knees. My full skirt fluffs out and covers my bent legs, her lap, and part of her stomach. I kneel over her. Only my inner knees and calves touch her. Her hands clasp my ass. She can feel through my skirt that I have no panties on. Her fingers search for the straps of my garter belt. She finds and gently unsnaps them. She rests her head, arched upward, against the sofa's back. A small puff of air, a slight moan, escapes her, the sound of someone tired from hard working. But her work hasn't begun yet.

She pulls me closer to her. Her fingers squeeze my ass. I grind my pubic bone against her, moving my hips then bending at the thigh, spreading my legs. I put the weight of my body on her lap. I rub my bare cunt against the cold metal of her belt buckle and then against her crotch. I wiggle and squirm, using her body as a point of friction for my erect nipples and lusty clit. I rub my breasts against her, licking and biting her neck and ears. I pinch her nipple through her T-shirt. I plunge my tongue into her mouth; my lips press hard against her flesh. Her hands move under my skirt, clasping my sensitive ass. I move my hips, pushing my wet cunt against her. *Fuck me,* my mind screams. *Fuck me now.*

I pull away, dismount, and position myself in the other corner of the sofa, fixing my skirt and smoothing my hair. She takes my hand and leads me to the bedroom. I see gleaming, twinkling, burning want in her eyes. My cunt is wet, my clit is warm, and a fire rages deep inside me. My nipples throb to be touched, pulled, bitten. I arrange myself diagonally on the bed, pulling my dress over my knees, crossing my legs at the ankles, leaning up on my elbows as she lights a few candles and dims the overhead lights. If I had refused to get off of the sofa, I wonder as I wait, watching her tight, small ass as she bends, would she have taken me there? Or would she have dragged me into the bedroom? The second answer appeals to me, and I toy with the image of her pulling me from the sofa, grabbing my hair, locking my neck in a wrestling hold, and dragging me, stumbling, into the bedroom. The film in my head skips, and I imagine her throwing me over her shoulder(my ass in the air, my legs kicking. Mmm. She stands in front of me, mischief in her eyes, looking at me. I examine her like she is a prize-winning animal: her slim body, slight hips, and tight little ass encased in a second skin of black leather pants; her small firm breasts; the curve of her shoulders; the bulging muscles of her upper arms, accented by a white tank top and leather suspenders; her feet, slightly apart in black biker boots with chain mail. I separate my lips as my eyes feast on her. Bold butchness oozes from her. I wonder if she can lift me onto her shoulder. I store the fantasy away for future use.

She lies next to me, slipping her arms around me. I collapse into her embrace as she kisses me. Submissive. Ready to be taken. Wanting, needing, and in heat. We move our hips against each other. Our tongues plunge roughly into each other's mouths. Her hand slides up my stocking-clad leg and under my skirt to my bare upper thigh. I clamp my hand around her wrist, stopping its progress. Her hand pushes to move forward; I do not yield. It concedes and allows me to guide it back to the outside of my dress, where I rest it on my waist and release it. We begin again. She nuzzles my breast and bites at the nipple through the material. I moan and grind my hips against the air. I want to feel her mouth on my bare flesh. I want her to pull my nipple rings and bite them as if she were removing the tip.

Her hand moves faster this time, pulling my skirt up and heading directly for my cunt. "No," I say sternly, as I clasp her wrist, pressing all my strength against her resistant arm. I am stronger than she thinks, but she is still stronger than I am. She could easily overpower me. Is she aware of this? Again she concedes, allowing me to lead her hand away from my wet cunt and back to my upper body. I begin to pull my skirt down. She firmly grabs my wrist, stopping me. This time I concede. I turn into her, grab the back of her head, pull it hard against my mouth, and kiss her deeply. I rub my exposed cunt, wet from want, against her leg, pushing hard so she can feel my pubic bone through her pants. I squirm against her, rubbing my erect nipples against her body. She cups my ass in her hands, pulling the cheeks up and slightly apart; her fingers dig into the bare flesh. She licks and bites my neck, groaning, growling. Her hips push against mine. My hips move against hers as I clasp and squeeze her butt cheeks. We simulate fucking, imitating the movement of penetration. I moan. I bite her neck, dig my nails into her arms, untuck her shirt, and run my nails up her back—first slowly and lightly, then faster and harder. Her arms clamp around my back, pinning my body against hers. My body says, *Fuck me; I want you.* I do anything I can to make her want to touch my wet cunt, to make her unable to control her want. Her hands are weak-willed; they plunge between my legs. This time I let her feel my wetness. I let her slip one finger deep inside me. She groans as her finger penetrates my flesh, separates the folds that cover my wet hole, and enters my cunt. I echo the groan as my cunt lips open and yield to her invasion. My wet, warm pussy engulfs her finger. She prods, stroking the walls of my cunt as my hips move to meet her. My senses slip from me. I cannot hear the music I know is playing.

This is dangerous. Ultimately, I am weak and my cunt is greedy. My cunt wants nothing more than to be fingered. Of course, sex doesn't only happen to my clit and cunt. Sex happens to my whole body. My flesh turns into one hot pulsating cunt, dripping wet with want. Sex happens in my head; my mind shifts as her lips, tongue, and teeth connect with my neck, mouth, or hand. Sex floods over me, crashes into a state of willing sexual accessibility. I go into heat like an animal. I will do anything for her to touch me, stroke me, fondle me, lick me, fuck me. Anything to make her not stop fucking me. My mind and cunt are constantly at war. My cunt lives for the moment, the very instant of orgasm, and my mind wants prolonged gratification(the rough, hard hour-long screw.

I try to exit the submissive, fuckable state of mind she forces me into. I know she'll put another finger in me soon, and then I'll belong to her. I must momentarily maintain control. I try to focus on the music before she completely consumes me with her skilled strokes. I grab her wrist. This time she refuses, using her superior strength and position on top of me. Instead of removing her fingers, she thrusts harder, deeper, using two, maybe three fingers, but I have other ways of stopping her. I slide my body up, using her shoulders for leverage, and detach myself from her hand. I squirm to get my legs out from under her before she regains control of my body.

Her eyes flicker, like a child robbed of candy. I meet her eyes: Their lust melts me. I want her to have me. *Fuck me,* my cunt screams, and it echoes through my whole body, causing a ripple of sensation that threatens to overwhelm me. I've paused momentarily in my escape, caught in my own desire to be overcome and forcibly fucked by her. She smells blood and jumps on me like a panther jumps on wounded prey. Her fingers press into my leg and arm as she twists my limbs to regain access to my cunt. I squirm, twist, and struggle to get away. She kneels by my feet, her body extended over me. Angry with myself for losing concentration, yet excited by the struggle, a wave of panic fills me. I put my foot against the knee she rests her weight on, pushing it from under her, forcing her to let go of me to regain her balance. I grab a handful of her hair, jerking her head back as I pull my body out from under her. She catches my ankles before I can slither off the edge of the bed, pulling me back and pinning me on my stomach, her body's weight across me. Her hands grasp my wrists and pin them to the bed. I buck against her, kick my feet frantically at her parted legs, push against her upper body, and try to lift my pinned arms. She bites the back of my neck and licks up to my ears. Her confidence in her ability to keep me pinned infuriates me—and makes me wetter. I struggle; she fondles my neck with her mouth. I cannot free myself. She knows this. I shriek in frustration. She whispers in my ear, "Why do you fight me? You are so wet, you want me to fuck you." Her words make my cunt hot. For a second, I almost give in to her: My muscles start to relax, and my body says, *Fuck me, take me, use my body as if you own me.*

Bitch, I say to myself, *how dare you confront me with my own lust, make me look it in the eye, and point to my desire to have your fingers deep inside me, your mouth on my clit. That top's trick may make me hot and weak, but it won't get you inside me.* I fight against my deep desire to submit to her touch; I push with all my strength, lifting us perhaps an inch, then collapse into the mattress.

She maneuvers my body, handling me like a feral cat. I allow my muscles to go limp so she can arrange me to be fucked. I wait for the opportunity, for the moment she carelessly grasps a leg as she reaches for a shackle, shifting her body weight, and becomes momentarily off-guard and off-balance. At that exact second, I quickly bring my free leg around, plant my platform fuck-me shoe between her breasts, tumble her back, and force her to release my body. I kick her chin, slamming her mouth shut. I squirm to my knees and prepare to jump off the bed, dash into the other room, and maneuver a piece of furniture between us.

She sits on her ass, her spread legs bent at the knees, her feet on the mattress. She runs the back of her hand across her mouth, looks at her own blood on her hand. Only her eyes move toward me. They lock on mine. Her normally soft and gentle blue eyes rage with fire, desire, need. They crackle, mesmerizing me. Hypnotized like a snake before a charmer, I cannot look away. I feel panic rising inside my chest. Her eyes say, *Now, now I will fuck you, penetrate you, slam you. Now I will have what I want from you. I will take it with force, and then you will beg me to give it to you again. You are mine, bitch.* Her eyes cause my clit to stir, and a wave of warm arousal mixes with the fear.

Without taking her eyes off mine, she licks the blood from her hand, and in a moment outside time, she lunges, grabs a fistful of my hair, pins me with her body, and forces my right arm into a leather cuff with a large silver buckle. I mouth the words, *No, please,* as I watch small drops of blood fall from her lips to my chest. I struggle as she cuffs the other wrist and attaches me to the O-ring mounted on the wall over the bed. I struggle in vain; the chain prevents me from going anywhere. She savagely pries my legs apart and plunges two fingers inside me. I moan, my hips thrust. I am as wet as if I had already come. She retreats, leaving me on my back.

Perhaps she will fist me, forcing my cunt to accept her whole hand; perhaps she will tease me until I beg her to make me come; or perhaps she'll fuck me with a dildo, plunging and slamming into me. It is beyond my control now. Whatever she does will fill the empty space inside me that started as a small yearning, eventually growing into a loud demand that must be sated. She must overcome, subdue, master, and fill my consuming hunger.

The hunger grows; it spreads away from my body and reaches toward her, its teeth exposed to rip her flesh. As she comes near me, her hand extending to grab my breast or neck, I flip onto my stomach and attempt to get on my knees. I will undo the chains from the O-ring and free myself. My upper body hits the mattress hard, facedown. My arms extend in front of me, my weight on my knees, my ass in the air. I feel my dress slide up and expose my bare ass. She licks between the crack and pushes hard with her tongue. The palm of her hand smacks my bare ass. I tighten the muscles at the second blow. I clasp my hands around the chains. The stinging begins. Her hand comes down, again and again, against my flesh. Her other arm encircles my hips, preventing me from sinking onto my stomach, forcing my exposed, quickly reddening ass to remain in the air, accessible and vulnerable. She stops. My ass stings, my cunt throbs, and my resistance has been consumed and replaced by hunger. Every part of me will submit to her touch. There is no resistance; I desperately want to be molded by her hands and tongue. The cells of my skin will yield to her touch and transform themselves into whatever she desires, as long as she touches them, touches me.

I feel pressure against my cunt lips. My own wetness has spilled out of me, basting my lips, betraying my desire. She does not use her other hand to separate and open me; there is pressure—intense and concentrated—against my cunt lips and a cool, slippery moisture that doesn't belong to me. I feel the head of the dildo slip forward and enter me, forcing my cunt to accept its size. It is too big. I stretch as the pressure continues. I moan, feeling a twinge of fear that I will rip. Pain stabs intensely as she pushes the head in, the slightly smaller shaft plunging in after it. My cunt is full; my back arches as the surge of pleasure rushes through me. She moves her hips slowly, working the shaft in and out of me. My cunt relaxes, submits to her invasion. The pain blends with the satisfaction of fullness. I slide into The Fuck. After a few full strokes in which the cock's shaft is consumed entirely by my cunt, her hips skip the steady climb and go from slow probing to slamming. Hard and fast, she plunges into me. Pounding away. Nailing me. Her sweat and the juices from my cunt cover us like baptismal water. The nerves in my vagina's soft flesh ache with sensation. Her thighs slap against my ass, her hand clutching my red ass as she slides, hard and fast, in and out of me. I am on my knees, my face against the mattress, my arms pulled tight. She pulls my ass toward her with each thrust.

I feel a popping sensation, followed by severe emptiness deep inside my cunt. My body is outraged; my hips stretch to follow her cock, but it isn't there. I groan with displeasure as she flips me onto my back, pushing my legs apart with her knees. There is no resistance in my muscles. Her hand pushes down on my pelvic bone. She reenters me with one strong full stroke. There is no resistance in my cunt. She fills the empty void. I am on my back, my legs in the air, my arms chained over my head to the wall. I see the top of her head, white-blond spikes dipped in black, sagging under the weight of sweat as her face presses into my chest. I see my own legs in black silk stockings, my six-inch fuck-me shoes bouncing on either side of her ass as she rams into me. She clamps her teeth on my nipple, pulling the ring, biting the flesh. I reach for her upper arms, but the chains stop my arms and prevent me from touching her. I want desperately to touch her arms, to sink my nails into her flesh, draw blood to the surface, free it as she frees me. The chains clank against each other. She thrusts into me deeper.

I dig my heels into her sides. She is a horse I ride. I want her to fuck me harder. I want her to fuck me so hard that her cock breaks through my organs, tears through the muscles, rips through the soft tissue of my belly, and pops out in a bloody fountain.

I know she can do it. I have faith in her ability to fuck, and I have felt the pure, raw animal in her. I believe our raw animal lust drives her. Her desire is fused to my need(she wants to make me relinquish my mind to her. She will do anything to push me into that blue, bottom space, to push me to the edge, to make me give her my orgasm.

"Harder," I gasp.

And she responds as if the idea had been her own. Perhaps it was. I am not sure where either of us ends or begins. Right now it doesn't matter. At this moment all that drives us is The Fuck. All that exists is The Fuck. I look into her face, her eyes closed, her arms tense and fully extended, holding her upper body above me. *Fuck me. Own me. I am yours to do with as you wish. Possess me. Consume me. Desecrate my body. Stab me there in that soft, sacred place, over and over. I will not resist you now. I will not refuse any request, any order, any demand, any desire.*

We are not two lesbians exploring each other's bodies; we are not two individuals. We are The Fuck, one consuming mound of carnal desires, impulses, raw primitive animal urges. Perhaps the desire to fuck harder, to plow deeper inside my wet, greedy cunt, was hers, and I was merely the vessel that gave voice to her need. Harder. Perhaps the want to be fucked harder, deeper, faster was mine, and the word never crossed my lips; it just issued from deep inside my snatch to her mind or muscles. I want her to fuck me, fill my whole body with her cock. Plow into my liver, kidneys, stomach. Push her cock through my uterus into my lungs. I want her to fill my whole body with its length and thickness, to spread the aching, throbbing pleasure that she is creating in my cunt throughout my body. I want her to pierce my heart and impale it on her cock, matching the rhythm of her fuck to the beats of my heart. I want her to fuck me until my eyes pop out and blood runs freely from my ears, nose, and mouth.

In one motion, her arms press my shoulders as she grabs me for more leverage, and her next downward stroke into my open cunt is harder than I had imagined possible. Her hips smack my upper thighs; her cock slides roughly in and out of me. The fake, stiff balls bump against my asshole, stirring a new emptiness, a new hole demanding to be filled. I clamp my legs around her, locking my ankles across her back. I shall never let go. My cunt and clit throb; my asshole stirs, demanding to be included. I want her to make me come, but I am a greedy slut. I don't want her to stop ramming her cock into me. I want to stay here, used and possessed by her hunger, locked together. I want to come before the fucking makes my clit explode, my mind implode. I cannot choose which I want—coming or prolonged possession. I cannot decide because I need both now. I want her to fuck me until I break, fuck me through the come, and not stop fucking me, fuck me until I die, fuck me until there is nothing left of me but a shell.

She makes the decision for me, removing the dildo from its ring, fucking me with it in her hand as her mouth engulfs my clit. Her tongue licks the engorged mass, flicking, pulling, putting pressure directly on it. I come, clamping her head between my legs, her mouth on my clit, her cock still slamming inside my cunt. She doesn't stop until the last spasm passes. My cunt and clit fuse; my entire being condenses to that one single point. She creates the moment of my consumption, erasing me completely. This is the moment she unravels me, undoes me, releases me. This is the moment I exist for; this moment is the only reason I am alive. This orgasm she has ripped from me— she owns it as much as I do. At this moment I do not exist. I am a nerve ending, an extension of her sexual desire. I am one large cunt and clit. She has forced this orgasm from me; she has created it from my resistance. She has reached deep inside me, letting my blood cover her hands as she tore through my liver, stomach, and heart and grasped my want, my sex, my power and pulled it to the surface—freeing it, freeing me. Even in this moment, my mind wonders what we will uncover inside me, what will come in the future, and what tools she will use to cut through my flesh, dig past my organs, and unearth the rest of me. For this moment is small; these acts merely touch the surface of the darkness we have tapped There is much still trapped inside me.

She collapses on top of me, sweating, breathing heavily. I gasp, trying to regulate my breath, pulling myself out of the euphoric mist she plunged me into. We lie there with our individuality returned to us—marked by The Fuck, changed by our exchange of sexual energies. I know she is wet under her harness, wet from possessing me, fucking me. The shy top in me yearns to engulf her cunt in my mouth, taste her wetness, plunge my fingers into her hole. I lie still, on my back, waiting for her to undo my shackles, as she kisses my neck. Even now, as I lie in her arms, both of us collapsed from exhaustion, my cunt is freed. It thinks about the next time. Next time, I'll scream so loud she'll have to gag me. Next time, I'll be stronger, hold out longer. Next time, she'll have to whip me into submission. Next time—she nuzzles her face into my chest, squeezing me slightly, then kisses my cheek—oh, next time, I'll be as weak as I was this time.

london calling

stefka

OK, chalk this up to a lapse of sanity. I had always thought of myself as a rational person, but when the plane landed in London, I realized I had finally lost my marbles. What did I think I was doing, traveling ten hours to a place I had never been, to meet someone I had only talked to on the phone and the computer? I needed to be locked up, and the key thrown away, because I would normally never do that. Yet, there I was, gathering my bag and my courage to meet a woman whose accent drove me batty, whose impish picture haunted my dreams. I had waited nearly a year to physically meet her, and now that the moment was upon me, I got a case of the nerves. There was no turning back now; I had a return ticket, but I would have to wait a week before I could use it, so I thought I might as well enjoy the week with someone I barely knew.

Baggage claim and customs took less time than I expected, even with my being American, and soon I found myself striding through the terminal with my heart in my throat. I spotted Michelle before she spotted me, and for a second, I stopped in my tracks. She looked exactly like her picture: her black hair short, her body tall and lanky. When her blue eyes finally spotted me, I was surprised by their size and vibrant color—the picture had only given a hint. Relieved and nervous, I pushed my cart over to her, and we smiled shyly at each other.

While we waited for the subway, or "tube," as she referred to it, we chatted nervously. Neither one of us knew what to do. It wasn't until we changed trains for the third time that we finally relaxed into easy conversation. After we reached the hotel and I deposited my bags, Michelle suggested we go out to get a bite to eat and drink. I eagerly agreed, only because the jet lag and my nerves played havoc with my body.

By the time I finished my drink at the third bar that night, I was ready to go back to the hotel. My body was tense, and my temples pounded from jet lag. I was exhausted. I looked over at Michelle, trying to catch her eye, but she was busy looking around, and I didn't want to draw attention to myself yet. Even though I wanted to sleep, I felt the familiar pull I always felt when I was in her company. Sitting with her in person was just as comfortable as chatting on the phone. I never wanted to leave once I had her attention, so I sat there, picked up my glass, and drank its dregs.

As I set the glass down, I saw two fresh drinks waiting, and I glanced at Michelle in surprise. She gave me a half-smile and motioned with her head. I squinted into the din but couldn't see what she was motioning to. Her smile widened.

She leaned forward, until her scent—a mixture of fresh flowers and soap—surrounded me as she fairly yelled in my ear over the loud music.

"Two blokes over there at the bar bought them."

I glanced over and caught sight of the two guys she meant. Frowning, I stared at the drinks, not really wanting another. I'd had enough at the second bar, my nerves having disappeared by the fourth drink. All I wanted now was someplace quiet, where I could listen to Michelle without outside interference.

She gave me a look I couldn't read, and nodded to the drinks. "You don't want it?"

I shook my head, pushing my empty glass next to the full one. Michelle nodded, set her empty glass down, and stood up. I followed her as she turned and said something to the server before heading to the door. My steps were quick, and I breathed a sigh of relief as the cool England air hit my heated face. She gave me another smile as she waved for a cab. I quickly slid inside when she opened the door, immediately resting my head on the worn vinyl seat and closing my eyes.

My headache was still there, but the fresh air had done it worlds of good, and I smiled as I slid along the seat as the car turned.

"Tired?" Michelle's voice, coated with her whirling accent, asked softly.

"Hmm, a little," I told her, not opening my eyes.

I was finally here, after nearly a year. It felt like a dream, a dream from which I definitely didn't want to wake up, at least not for the week I would be there. I fought sleep because I didn't want to miss a thing, but I must have dozed off, because I felt Michelle gently shake my shoulder when the car stopped.

"We're here."

I gave her a sheepish grin, waiting until she got out before sliding across the seat to follow her outside. When I looked around, I realized we were back at the hotel, and I was surprised to find myself a little disappointed that our first day would end so soon. But I said nothing as we entered the lobby together, and we went to the elevator without speaking a word.

I watched as Michelle punched the button for our floor. She gave me a sidelong glance as I leaned against the wall, suddenly wide awake, my body tingling all over. It had to be the jet lag; it just had to be. I tensed slightly when the bell announced our arrival by a soft tinkling. The doors whooshed open, and we walked to our room, where I slipped out of my jacket and tossed it on a chair before raising my arms in a stretch, my muscles cramped.

I hadn't even lowered my arms when a hand seized my hair, rudely turning me around. Startled, I made no move to resist, letting the hand maneuver me to face my assailant. My eyes widened when I caught sight of Michelle's dark ones. I felt her hand tremble, even though it gripped my short hair tightly. Her face flushed, and her breathing became rapid. Instead of fighting her, or even trying to remove her hand, I watched her to see what she would do next.

I found myself up against the wall, thrown with amazing strength. I landed with a loud thud, my head ringing. For some reason, I wasn't frightened, and I didn't curse. I straightened up, then crouched defensively, a wide smile creasing my face. I geared myself for a pounce, but she anticipated me and pounced instead, pinning me against the wall. Her hands gripped my wrists, pushing them over my head as she gripped them tightly. I automatically flexed, and she pressed hard against me. I smiled.

She was strong, her heart hammering against my chest as she looked at me, her eyes dark and wicked. I found her fierce gaze appealing, and I arched against her. She growled deeply and pressed even harder, my head banging against the wall again. She had me pinned. I could have broken away, but I didn't. I wanted to see what she wanted or needed.

She buried her face in my neck and gripped me with her teeth, nipping my sensitized skin. I arched my neck against her mouth, moaning in pleasure. She trailed her mouth along my neck until we came face-to-face again, her mouth open slightly as her chest heaved against mine.

"Tired?" she demanded, her voice low and soft, her tone firm.

I swallowed hard before grinning. "Fuck no." She flashed a smile before moving her head and capturing my lips with hers.

The kiss was rough, and slightly painful. I waged battle with her demanding tongue, enjoying her control but not ready to give in completely. I returned her kiss, bringing her bottom lip into my mouth with my teeth, pinching her. She pressed her body closer, grinding her hips against me as her knee shoved its way between us.

Her hand released mine, and I immediately grabbed it as it trailed roughly along my front, clutching my breasts as her fingers pinched my hard nipples through my shirt. Harsh moans surrounded us, creating a music all its own, and I became faint with pent-up desire. I had imagined our first time together—we had spoken of it often enough—but this was not at all what I had imagined. I throbbed with need.

Michelle gripped my shirt and ripped it open, buttons flying as she quickly pushed aside my sports bra and clamped her teeth on a tender nipple. She chewed roughly as her tongue jerked one nipple ring. She took her time mauling my breasts, her teeth tugging on the chain between my rings as she went back and forth between my nipples. Her hands were busy as well, one pulling the chain while the other raked along my side until it reached the waistband of my jeans. She fumbled for a second, then opened the fly and yanked my jeans and underwear to my ankles.

I was exposed, wet and needy—and she knew it. As her teeth continued to ruin my nipples, her hand found me, her fingers rough and firm as she rubbed my swollen clit in fast motion. I immediately arched under her hand, growling and banging my head against the wall as I flattened my hands against it to brace myself. I had no control; I could barely move to stop her; my body was on fire with need. Her hand knew exactly what I wanted—she slipped two fingers inside me and pounded away as she continued to bite and chew my nipples.

Sweat coated my skin as she lowered herself to her knees,

covering my clit with her mouth as her hand continued to ram me. My hips arched away from the wall, but my shoulders remained glued. My throat bobbed as I tried to say something, but only harsh grunts came out as she increased her pace and pressure until finally I stood on my tiptoes, trembling. She planted her other hand on my hip and pressed her face closer, lapping me up.

I nearly jumped out of my skin when I felt her teeth take my tender clit between them and chew it as she had with my nipples. As one release faded another built, and I knew I was in trouble as she increased the pumping even more. Her teeth and lips ate me; I was a fresh kill for an animal. Her groans and growls vibrated through me, and I thrashed my head as my hands fluttered against the wall. My throat hurt from my harsh groans, but I couldn't stop their fall from my lips. Her hand crept behind me, gripping my ass painfully as she continued to pump, bruising me the most delicious way possible.

Finally, when I knew I couldn't take it anymore, when Michelle took pity on me, she slammed my hips, her arm ramming into me one final time, then let me go. My throat burned in a howl, her name barely audible in the noise as I tumbled. Once the immense, powerful feeling left my body, I was nothing but mush. I slid down the wall, unable to hold myself up.

Michelle lay across my lap, her breathing as harsh as mine. She raised her hand and tugged on my nipple chain again, no less roughly than the first time, and I felt the familiar stirring once more. I swallowed hard before bending down and yanking her hair.

"So much for sleep," I growled.

"I was hopping you would say that." She tugged even harder at the chain.

I could do nothing by growl louder. I was no less gentle with her, using her body as she had used mine. I ate her and fucked her until we collapsed on the floor, sweating and heaving. Every time we mentioned a shower, one of us started in on the other, until the thought disappeared from our minds. I finally got to sleep just as the sun crested the sky. Jet lag, exhaustion, and pleasure had shut my body down.

I never saw her after that week. We both knew it wouldn't have worked out—living in two different countries made things too difficult. I still think I was a little insane for flying out there to see her, but I'm glad I did, because when I think of London, I think of her.

a very special israeli souvenir

●

rachel kramer bussel

December 31, 1996: I was in Israel on a two-week college student trip. We were all virgin visitors to the Holy Land, young Jews learning about our heritage and history. We'd done some socializing but were mostly busy being tourists, visualizing our ancestors walking the same lands thousands of years ago. But that night was a break from our more serious pursuits. We were in Tel Aviv, ready to venture to a local nightclub and celebrate the New Year, an outing for which I'd come utterly unprepared.

While my trip mates dolled themselves up with fancy designer makeup and even fancier dresses and shoes, I donned the only thing I could find that was even remotely suitable: a faded sheer dress that hung loosely around my body. When I say "sheer," I don't mean "sexy" like lingerie. I mean pale, faded soft cotton fabric that resembled a washrag. Since the dress was so sheer, I wore jeans underneath, completing my disaffected antifashion look. And off we went.

We arrived at the club, which was full of European and American tourists, with a few Israelis. Music by Madonna and the Spice Girls assaulted our ears. One of my friends bought me a drink, which had so much rum I had to hand it back. I'm not a teetotaler by any means, but I need a little sweetness in my drinks (and my women). We proceeded to stake out our own little area in the back and boogied. I pretended I had on the most glamorous outfit ever and shook my ass with the rest of the crowd. My eyes were closed, and my hair flew everywhere as I lost myself in the music.

I was so into the blaring beats that I barely noticed the slim, blond girl who wiggled her way through the crowd to our area. I saw her rebuff two of the more macho members of my group and thread her way next to me. She was only inches away, staring at me as she gyrated her hips. She seemed to be flirting with me, but I couldn't be sure. I continued my own gyrations and waited to see what would happen. I didn't have to wait long; the next thing I knew, she was running her fingers down my arm, smiling into my face. I smiled back and slithered into her arms; if a hot girl wanted to dance with me, who was I to say no?

We danced close like that for a few songs before she pulled my face to hers and kissed me deeply, her tongue swirling into my mouth, leaving my whole body weak.

"Do you like girls?" she yelled over the music.

"Yeah," I said casually.

"Really?"

"Yes. Don't you believe me?" I grabbed her ass and pulled her next to me so I could suck on her ear.

She stepped back and waved her hand in front of me, showing off a sparkling diamond ring. "I just got married five days ago," she said proudly.

Her statement puzzled me, but if she was happy about being married and still wanted me, I wasn't going to worry about it.

I felt my fellow travelers eyeing us with envy, so we moved to another part of the club. I met her husband, who scurried off to buy us drinks. Her body was so compact, her breasts pushed together under her tight white top. I leaned forward and nuzzled my face in her cleavage, while she tossed her head back and reveled in my explorations. We kissed passionately, holding on to each other as our tongues mingled, our bodies buzzing with sexual energy. It was like a dream—something that happens in movies, or to someone else, but not to frumpy old me, who had to be dragged to the club. I wondered briefly why she'd chosen me, but I brushed that thought from my mind as her hand squeezed my ass through my jeans.

"You're really turning me on. Do you know that?" I groaned into her ear.

She smiled at that, a big grin that told me she knew exactly what she was doing.

Guys approached, pestering us to join our little lovefest. My admirer shunted them off. She was so open with her lust, a refreshing change from going to clubs and eyeing a girl all night, only to go home alone before either of us worked up the courage to speak to each other. She kissed me ravenously, squeezing and stroking my body as her tongue worked its way around my mouth. She brought her lips to my neck, sliding her tongue along my sweaty skin and causing a mini earthquake in my cunt.

As she planted kisses all over me, I thought, *Who knew Israeli women were so wild?* I'd been hearing about Israel my entire life, but as a state of righteous political drama, with Zionists staking their claim for the rights of Jews everywhere. Now I had an Israeli girl, blond and pale like me, staking her claim on my body. She twisted my preconceived notions around as easily as her fingers twisted my nipple beneath my dress.

Her husband finally returned, and though he seemed like a nice person, a threesome wasn't really what I had in mind. It was quite late by now, several hours into the New Year, and as the Spice Girls sang, "If you wanna be my lover, you gotta get with my friends," I bid them adieu. From that point on, my classmates looked at me with envy and respect, and I took my memory of that night home as a very special Israeli souvenir.

the favor

●

sydney larkin

The Chicago show was shaping up to be more trouble than it was worth. I had hesitated to take the rigging job with this out-fit in the first place, but a bunch of their regular roadies were in Europe with another show, so they were desperate and therefore paying well. I reminded myself of that fact when I discovered we weren't in Chicago at all; we were across the border in Kenosha, Wisconsin. Nothing against Wisconsin, but when someone told me one of our gigs was in Chicago, I was a little surprised to end up in Kenosha instead.

The site turned out to be a muddy high school football field, just off the interstate, with nothing around but a dilapi-dated Days Inn and a questionable food-and-drink establish-ment called the Brat Stop. The June weather was downright crappy for a girl used to Southern California's mild summers. The sun would burn for hours; then the rain would explode without warning. The night before, a surprise thunderstorm had destroyed much of our stage setup, which had taken two days to erect. I didn't look forward to building it again. And it was only the fourth stop on the tour—twenty-two more to go.

Surveying the field at five in the morning, I realized the

damage was mostly superficial. Only one of the frames on which a banner was rigged had been permanently bent. The others had merely been knocked out of place by the wind. Everything was still soaking wet and filthy. *Should be able to get this in shape in plenty of time,* I thought.

I wasn't the only one at the site early. The other riggers, sound guys, and stagehands were milling around, trying to decide how to start the recovery effort. I walked over to David, the crew captain. "Anything serious?" I asked.

"Nope," he said. "No permanent damage. But it did just enough to make the whole day a pain in my ass."

No kidding, I thought. *This whole gig is a pain in my ass.*

I walked back toward the destroyed metal frame, past the merchandising trailers set up on the field's left side. The marketing crew was nowhere to be seen, probably sleeping in. *The sponsors are going to be really pissed if their precious merchandising trailers aren't spotless and shiny by noon,* I thought. *Oh, well, not my problem.*

I focused on trying to build a new frame by piecing spare parts together from the stash I kept in my truck. After a couple hours, I had everything in place except for one missing elbow joint. I wandered over to the main supply truck to see if I could snake an extra one from the materials manager. As Jim walked the shelves looking for the joint, I sat on the edge of the truck, took off my hat, and lit a cigarette. I inhaled deeply, closed my eyes, and let the newly risen sun heat my face.

"Well, I'll be," Jim said from behind me.

"What's that?"

"Those marketing folks decided to show up after all," he replied.

I opened my eyes and saw four figures walking toward the merchandising trailers. I recognized the swagger of Kevin, the manager. He could talk anyone into buying the cheap T-shirts, key chains, and other trinkets they hawked. The rest of the crew thought of the marketing team as a bunch of lazy free-loaders, and Kevin did nothing to combat that impression.

"Fucking princesses." Jim shook his head with disgust. "I know they bring in revenue, but those four are completely use-less when it comes to the real work of getting the show up and running. I can't believe they call themselves roadies. It's bad for morale."

I tended to agree. I looked at the ruined field, the stage's steel truss supporting the precariously hanging video screen. Slowly, some tough stagehands raised it back into position. I glanced back to the four people polishing the merchandising trailers' chrome ramps. *What a joke.* I chuckled to myself and took a last drag on my cigarette.

For a moment I imagined what it would be like not to worry about heavy lights and poles falling on people's heads, instead worrying about how pretty a stupid merchandise counter looked. I saw a hand work a cloth over the trailer's shiny metal. It was a surprisingly strong looking hand, with long, lean fingers entering the grooves of the diamond plate–floor. A muscular forearm soon appeared, displaying toned biceps and triceps. The smooth skin strained against a tight T-shirt that hid the well-defined shoulder. The shirt rose slightly with each sweep of the cloth, drawing attention to a long, graceful neck. The neck was powerful and feminine. Suddenly, I was keenly aware how long it had been since I'd had the pleasure of touching a beautiful woman.

"Sure wouldn't kick that JD out of bed."

Jim's comment jerked me out of my fantasy as he caught me staring. I tried to refocus.

"But I have it on good authority that she plays for your team, sport. I'm out of luck." He grinned and put something in my hand. "Here's your elbow. Good luck."

He winked, and I felt my face redden as I took the piece of metal pipe.

I'd heard rumors about JD's sexuality, and she had certainly set off my gaydar, but despite our occasional conversations
and the fact of living on the same touring bus, we never got
beyond a surface interaction. She was always friendly but definitely shy and intensely private about her personal life. I made
an automatic assumption that a woman who kept her company so closely guarded wouldn't be interested in an obvious
dyke like me.

An hour later, I finished attaching the dirty banners to the
new frame as a voice behind me asked, "Are you going to have
those cleaned in time?"

"I will as long as everything stays dry," I said, turning
around. I immediately knew that would never happen, as I felt
hot liquid pool between my legs.

JD stood before me in her tight T-shirt and cutoffs, looking
as hot as ever despite dirt smudges on her arms and face. I
couldn't help but notice the way her jeans hugged the curve of
her hips, accentuating her thigh muscles. Knowing I had taken
too long to make eye contact, I deliberately forced my eyes
upward, over her torso's soft lines, across her collarbone's
sharp sexy protrusion, up to her full lips and high cheekbones,
until I locked eyes with her. She smirked, unself-conscious
about my frank appraisal, meeting my gaze intensely.

"I have a feeling that nothing's going to be dry for a while,"
she said, moving closer and running her hand over the mesh
banner. "Is there anything I can do to help?"

"No. I think I have everything under control," I said.

"Oh, I'm sure you do. You always seem to. But if you decide
you need a favor, just remember I'm available."

She turned and walked away. I was shell-shocked by the erotic energy we had just exchanged, but I quickly attributed it to
my own sex drive. JD was simply interested in giving me a hand.

Or a whole fist, my libido hoped.

The show went off without a hitch. We struck the majority

of the site that night but weren't scheduled to move to the next city until the following evening.

A hypothetical scenario: thirty-six roadies in a rural area with one hotel and one bar, leaving the next day for another eighteen weeks of life on a bus, given permission to get the sleep the previous day's storm had denied them, allowed to return in the morning instead of working through the night. Needless to say, sleep was not at the top of our agenda.

I was on my third beer at the Brat Stop, and had my name on the chalkboard in line to play pool, when JD sauntered over.

"Any interest in a friendly game of air hockey while you wait to destroy these poor boys at pool?"

Her olive skin, deeply tanned by hours spent in the sun, looked even darker against her crisply pressed white shirt. The top three buttons were unbuttoned, affording me an intriguing view of her cleavage. I'd already been waiting forty-five minutes to get on the table, and since her perfume danced seductively in my nose, I couldn't think of a single reason not to accept her challenge.

"Sure," I replied.

As I scrounged up quarters from the depths of my jeans pockets, I regarded her. "Why do I not quite believe you when you say this is going to be a friendly game?"

"Well, things can definitely be friendly, but they're never free. There needs to be a stake involved."

She obviously felt no pain, and for a moment I wondered if it was ethical to pursue a serious wager in such a scenario. I decided to leave the ball in her court.

"What shall we play for?" I asked.

She held my eyes for a beat before responding. "How about a favor? It can be anything, redeemable at any mutually agreeable time."

Her eyes bored into me, and for the second time that day I felt blood rush to my most sensitive lips. As much as my mind said this was a bad idea, it was hardly the most vocal body part as I made the decision.

"Fine with me," I heard myself say. "Let's go."

Half an hour later, the score was tied three games to three, and we were halfway through the seventh game. I was well into my fifth beer, and quite frankly all I could think about was the way JD's fingers grasped the mallet and the way her arm muscles flickered when she took a shot. I blamed this distraction for my four-to-three loss. After some pointed looks and a lot of drunken innuendo, I stumbled across the street and back into my hotel room, now owing JD "a favor."

Life's tough, I know.

I managed to grab a couple hours of sleep and get back to the field on time in the morning. We were due to complete the breakdown and go back to our rooms for showers by 7 P.M. so the buses could leave for Cleveland by 10.

The rest of the breakdown was uneventful. I kept looking for JD out of the corner of my eye but knew she and the rest of the marketing team had no reason to be on-site, as they had finished their work shortly after the show ended. But thoughts of her eyes, and the games the night before, made the day go by faster. As I worked, I fantasized about the amazing and varied things her hands could do to me, the way her naked body would feel against mine, the way her face would look when she came... *Stop it*, I told myself. *Never going to happen. She was just drunk and having fun, and you're making too much out of it. And now you're horny as hell, just in time to board a bus filled with eight other people, no privacy, and a coffin-size bunk for a bed. Well done, way to go.*

We packed the trucks in record time, and most of us were on our respective buses by 8:30. As always, our driver, Andy, had taken care of us by stocking our small kitchenette with snacks, sandwich fixings, the occasional piece of fruit, and of course, beer and other alcohol.

I was the last to arrive on my bus, and Andy was right behind me with orders to move out once everyone was accounted for. By the time I situated myself and prepped my bunk for the night's trip, we were rolling down the interstate toward Ohio.

The rest of my bus mates were already in the throes of a mini party. It had been such a hellish stop on the tour that I only wanted to sleep and put Kenosha behind me, but I knew no one would let me off that easy. My best move, I thought, was to wait out the drunken revelry until everyone passed out.

The boys had the back lounge's television tuned to a ridiculous soft-porn flick, so I moved to the front lounge, where the entertainment fare was a recent action blockbuster. I grabbed a beer from the fridge, cracked it open, and sat down at the table. Surveying my colleagues, it was clear that waiting them out wouldn't take too long. I was calculating how many days it would be before I had the privacy of my own hotel room again when JD sat down across from me.

"They have a huge head start," she said, pointing to my beer. "You'll never catch up."

I smiled and took another sip. "I was looking forward to a mellow trip, but that's not going to happen. I'm just out here for fear of getting dragged out of my bunk if I try to go to bed. And I'm pretty sure they won't let me change the channel either. So I'd rather just nurse this puppy and stare out the window until they calm down."

She grinned. "How about some cards?"

"Now there's a wholesome pastime."

"Maybe not so wholesome," she said, winking and handing me a deck. I fanned the cards. The backs displayed naked 1950s pinup girls.

"I'd never peg you as a fan of the girlie magazines."

"Well, there's a lot you don't know about me. Go get another drink and we'll play gin."

I crossed the aisle to the kitchen cabinet. Swayed by the game's suggestive name, I found the nearly full bottle of Bombay Sapphire and poured myself a healthy slug. *This could get interesting*, I thought as I put the bottle back on the shelf.

Two hours and many drinks later, our rowdy bus mates had retired to their bunks to sleep off their party. JD and I were still having a grand old time playing cards, having switched from gin to go fish after the third hand. Despite the game's laughter and silliness, I couldn't help noticing JD's well-manicured nails and long slender fingers. I also couldn't stop the throbbing between my legs as I imagined what those fingers might feel like inside me.

"Smoke?" Once again, she had caught me amidst inappropriate thoughts.

I was grateful for the easy question. "Absolutely."

We made our way to the very front of the bus, stumbling slightly. We pushed the curtain aside and sat down on the entry stairs next to Andy.

"Hey, ladies. I thought you'd be in bed long before those yahoos ever crashed out."

"I think I'll be there soon," I replied, accepting the lighter from JD. "I'm beat."

We chatted with Andy as we smoked. JD's shoulder touched mine, and I felt the heat of her eyes every time she looked my way. *I'd better get out of here or I'm going to get myself in trouble*, I thought.

Just as I was about to retire for the evening, I felt my right sock slip off my foot. I turned to see JD dangling it in front of me.

"Are you really going to go to bed with only one sock?" Her words were slightly slurred, but her eyes were clear and intense, sending an electric shock straight to my clit. Caught off guard, I stretched forward for my sock. JD whipped the sock behind her back, out of my reach, and I fell against her. I tried to pull back, but she grabbed the back of my head, pushing my face into her neck. I was still a little confused—until I felt her nails dig into my back and I heard her sigh softly. The sock forgotten, I moved my hand to her stomach and stroked it gently. Her hips arched toward me; her thighs parted.

"Wait," she breathed. "Andy's right there. We should go back to the lounge."

I released her, and she headed into the lounge. I followed, and as I drew the curtain I saw Andy's lips curve into a smirk. *Eyes on the road, buddy*, I thought.

The door to the bunks was closed, but there was only a thin curtain between the lounge and Andy, so I popped a CD in the stereo and turned it up. JD had tossed a pillow and a blanket onto one of the couches, and she stood in the kitchen dimming the lights. I walked toward her, wrapped my arms around her from behind, and kissed the back of her neck.

"I need to take my contacts out," I mumbled.

She turned around and pushed me against the refrigerator. "Uh huh," she said, pinning my shoulders with her hands and grinding her pelvis into mine. "You go ahead and do that."

Any possible response was quickly silenced by her mouth on mine. Not at all gentle, her tongue probed my mouth, and her teeth bit my lips. I couldn't move, couldn't breathe. I was swept away by her forcefulness. Shy indeed! This woman had the sexual inhibition of a dominatrix.

She let up for a moment, just long enough to maneuver me to the couch. Pushing me down, she tore off my other sock, unzipped my pants, and slid them over my hips as I yanked my shirt off. She made quick work of my bra and underwear, and I shortly found myself pinned again, this time underneath her.

Her mouth was relentless, demanding the full attention of everything it touched. Her hands ran over my torso, grabbing my breasts and pinching my nipples. Her tongue moved down my neck, teeth nibbling here and there, stopping randomly to bite fully, making me moan. When her mouth reached my breasts she took a nipple between her teeth, and I gasped. Each exquisite twinge of pain sent shockwaves to my clit, a rush of hot liquid pooling between my legs.

A hand slid down my inner thigh, working its way toward my cunt excruciatingly slowly. My hips had a mind of their own, thrusting toward her, trying to hurry the inevitable contact. My breath came quickly, the hairs on the back of my neck stood up, and my clit felt like it would explode.

She gasped when her fingers finally found my inner lips. "Oh, my God, you are so fucking wet," she breathed as she slid two fingers inside me. My muscles clamped around her fingers as she started to slowly move in and out of me. Every nerve ending tingled in anticipation as her head continued its journey down my body. When her mouth finally paused between my spread legs, her hot breath flowed over my hair. She was millimeters from me.

"Please," I moaned, looking down at her.

She met my eyes with a teasing look of her own, inhaling my scent deeply. "You smell so good," she said, before moving closer.

When the tip of her tongue touched my hardened nub, I cried out in pleasure. She moved slowly, simultaneously enveloping my entire clit in her mouth and flicking its tip with her tongue. Her fingertips continued to massage my inner muscles as her tongue worked my clit expertly.

As I went out of my mind with ecstasy, she coordinated her rhythms with the bucking of my hips. The throbbing of my cunt drowned out the music from the stereo and the sound of the road. I felt a tingling orgasm approaching faster than I wanted, but I could do nothing to stop it.

"Yes, yes, yes, please," I cried, as waves of pleasure swept over me.

She didn't move away at first but stayed with her tongue against my clit, moving it incrementally to cause orgasmic aftershocks. "I can feel you contracting around my fingers," she said. "It's so damned sexy."

I was in the process of getting myself together to return the favor when she murmured, "I don't think you're quite finished."

She started moving inside me, sliding her fingers out then in again, causing my hips to react again, matching the increasing speed. I moaned, unable to keep a clear thought in my head.

"You need more than this, don't you?" she asked as she moved to her knees. She slid a third finger into me and began to move faster and faster until she thrust with all of her strength.

"Oh, God, yes, fuck me! Faster, harder, oh, yes!" I was a madwoman, thrashing about and moaning. "I'm going to come all over the couch."

"Go ahead, it's OK," she cooed as she thrust into me harder. "I want to feel you all over my hand."

Her words excited me even more, and I stopped worrying about the couch, the bus, Andy—anything other than what she was doing to me. Her fingertips found the right place inside me and suddenly a deluge of liquid poured out of me. I screamed, grabbing her shoulders, pulling her on top of me.

"I've never seen anything like that before," she said once my breathing calmed. "The couch is soaked."

I laughed weakly. "I tried to warn you. I wasn't kidding around."

"I loved it. It was spectacular."

"*You* were spectacular. I had no idea you had it in you," I said as I pushed her to the floor.

"I told you there was a lot you didn't know about me," she replied.

"Like what you look like under those clothes?" I asked as I unbuttoned her shirt.

I awoke on the floor of the lounge near dawn, naked and alone. The bus was still moving, and everything was quiet. I grabbed my clothes and stumbled back to my bunk. I crawled inside, but not before I pulled back JD's curtain to see if she was there. She was, sleeping soundly, with the same distinctive smile she had on her face when she came.

That was the only time we got together, as the sponsors cut the marketing staff when we got to Cleveland and sent the four of them home. JD and I lost touch, but I'll never forget that overnight bus trip. And neither will the others on the tour, thanks to Andy. He said he found something more compelling to listen to as he drove that night, instead of his book on tape.

He also brought the mirror on the front lounge's ceiling to my attention. Damn, I'd completely forgotten. Guess I'll just have to take advantage of that next time I have to pay back a favor.

the lesson

stefka

For the millionth time I asked myself what the hell I was doing. Why was I driving over to a straight woman's house to fix her dinner? For the millionth time, the little voice in my head said calmly, "To teach her a lesson." The response was reasonable enough, and I often nodded because I partly agreed, but I also worried I was setting myself up for something I normally abhorred: playing with someone's heart. I think one reason I'd agreed to dinner in the first place was because I'd had my heart broken three times by straight women who thought they wanted to be gay but in the end felt the "lifestyle was too much to handle."

I snorted; the sound echoed through my truck cab. "Lifestyle," they called it… What the hell did they know? It isn't a lifestyle, like living as a millionaire or even as a middle-class suburbanite. It's a way of life, meaning a person can't be anything except who they are, but try explaining that to people outside the circle and they roll their eyes and walk away. Maybe it was my ego that urged me to give Rachel my number, and maybe it was also the reason I accepted the dinner date two days later. I was tired of people telling me it was wrong to be who I was and I wanted to show everyone, including Rachel, what it was like to be me.

I shifted in my seat, merging onto the highway toward Deception Pass and my ultimate destination, Rachel's house. My parents lived on the island, as had I off and on for the past ten years, so I knew where I was going. I rubbed my face, reaching over and turning up the stereo volume to block out my thoughts, but nothing doing. They wouldn't leave me alone.

It all started when I went to a party with a friend of mine— a type of party I wouldn't usually attend. Margo, my friend, frequented a place called Freak Manor, a place where people, gay or straight, would go to enjoy themselves without being censored. Brightly colored hair, dog collars, and nudity were the norm in this place. There was even a playroom, affectionately called "the dungeon," only it was much danker. People were crammed onto every available surface suitable for sitting in the sparsely furnished house, and I felt uncomfortable, but since my friend was moving across the country two days later I figured, *What the hell.* Normally, if I wanted to be with that kind of crowd, it would be a little more controlled, with the host at least visible. "Unique individuals" overran the place, and I felt completely out of place. For the next five hours I found myself in a crowded room with people I didn't know while Margo, laughing and having a good time, flitted in and out. I was bored, and after another hour had passed, I figured it was time to locate my ride and head home.

As I gathered my leather coat, in walked three people: two girls and a guy. Rachel, Catrina, and Bryan were announced to the group. I rolled my eyes as the two girls promptly kissed. They fairly screamed straight, yet they were trying to pass themselves off as queer. As I tried to figure out how to leave gracefully, one of the girls decided to sit next to me. OK, not next to me— practically on my lap. It was as if she hadn't seen me sitting there or hadn't noticed there was plenty of room on the couch. Calmly, she plopped her cute ass right on my leg and only moved slightly away when she realized I wasn't part of the decor.

I have to admit, she was rather appealing to look at, with her long, curly copper hair, pretty face, and large blue eyes. Her black skirt hugged her lower half nicely, and her black and red blouse revealed her big boobs, but that wasn't enough to keep me sitting there. Finally, she looked at me and smiled. Dimples peeked from both sides of her full lips, while her baby blues blinked cutely at me. Instead of leaving, I engaged her in conversation. It was the only polite thing to do, and if I had learned nothing else from my mother, I had acquired manners.

I enjoyed myself, flirting with her as she had flirted with me. She introduced herself as Rachel, and she seemed innocent and sweet, but she rubbed her hands up and down my thighs, asking if it was all right with me, saying that she was "just a tactile person, and loved the feel of leather." Yeah, right...she was a crafty minx, and she was testing me. But it was working, getting me hot and wet—that is, until her friend, the one she had kissed, revealed she was married. A cold shower couldn't have stopped my rising libido as fast as that little statement. I knew my first impression had been right: They were straight, and I didn't want anything to do with them. I wasn't about to be another experiment for anyone, and I vehemently said so. Once again Rachel surprised me as she passionately told me she adored women, remarking that she was basically bisexual but preferred women. Normally I didn't have a problem with bisexuals, but at the time it bothered me that she was married, yet she was caressing my leg. She claimed she was lonely with her husband being out to sea for six months and wanted another woman to be close to. I flatly told her she was using that excuse because she wanted to have her cake and eat it too. We had a heated discussion about that for the next hour or so until her friend decided it was time to leave. I can't explain how it happened, but before I knew what I was doing, I whipped out a piece of paper and quickly jotted down my number before giving it to Rachel with a cheerful smile. I figured I could show her that a "preference" for women might make her more than bisexual. She took my number, told me she would give me a call sometime, and departed with her friends. I waited for another hour before I finally got up and left, leaving my friend to enjoy herself.

She called at six that morning, and twice again that night, before we finally set a date: I would come over to fix her dinner. I think that was the real reason she called. I was a chef, and she loved to eat, as she told me when we met, although her body certainly didn't illustrate that fact. She wanted a private show of my talents, and I figured, what the hell, I'd show her all of my skills—including the bedroom ones.

So there I was, driving to Rachel's house, knowing full well from past experience that she would do everything in her power to entice me into her bed. But I had every intention of showing her what a "real" lesbian could do. She was going to get the show of a lifetime, and I would have the satisfaction of showing her what being toyed with felt like. I wasn't about to let myself fall for Rachel, although I did like our conversations, and her looks were pretty pleasant. But my heart was steel, and nothing could penetrate its armor, not even a cute little married woman with a killer smile.

Just as I thought, her house was easy to find, and just as I figured, she wasn't even dressed yet. She opened the door in a pale blue robe, with a pink towel wrapped around her head. She gave me an apologetic smile, showed me to her room, and proceeded to get dressed. She showed no shyness when she dropped her robe on the floor, letting me get a look at her perfectly round breasts. She slipped into a pair of black slacks before covering those gorgeous globes with a bra and blue top.

Me, I was the perfect gentlewoman. I didn't gape or stare. Instead, I lay flat on Rachel's bed, staring at the ceiling while she combed her glorious hair and put on makeup. We chatted about nothing while she got ready, and I wondered if I had been wrong about her. Maybe she was just lonely—with her husband out to sea and few friends since she had only recently moved to the island. Maybe she wasn't interested in having sex with a lesbian after all. Maybe she just wanted a nice meal. Right.

I thought I would test my theory in the car while we drove to the local grocery store. "Rachel," I began as I glanced at her cute profile, "what would you say if I told you I wanted to kiss you right now?"

She shot me a startled look. She didn't answer until we were in the parking lot. "Well, thank you for the thought, but I really don't want to go there right now."

I was a little disappointed by her answer, but it revealed I had been wrong after all. All she wanted was dinner. I relaxed a little, and we went into the store—where she decided to hang all over me like I was a coatrack as we gathered ingredients from the aisles. She was playing with me after all! She had said no, yet she hugged me, touched me, and crawled into my skin. What kind of game was she playing?

It didn't end there. When we returned to her house, it got worse. Rachel hovered over my shoulder as I started making dinner. She licked my fingers whenever I had butter, garlic, oil from the sun-dried tomatoes, or anything remotely wet on my fingers. They weren't just quick licks either. Oh, no! She had my insides clamoring for more as my pussy dripped from her ministrations. Christ, the woman knew how to use her tongue!

When we finally sat down to eat, she dug into my pasta dish, laced with shrimp, salmon, garlic, and sun-dried tomatoes, as if it were her last meal. She made little moaning sounds after each bite, driving my oversensitive hormones wild. No one had ever reacted to my cooking like that. I honestly thought Rachel was having mini orgasms with each bite. I could barely eat; I was riveted to her face. I watched her every move as she lifted her fork, pasta and shrimp speared on the small prongs, and inwardly groaned to see her lovely face expressing joy as she chewed each morsel. *What have I gotten myself into?* I thought as my eyes hungrily watched her eat.

I was a mess by the time we finished eating. I had to go to the bathroom to wipe my own juices. Whatever Rachel's game was, my poor body enjoyed it. My mind, on the other hand, told me to screw the lesson I supposedly wanted to teach her and get the hell out of there. Did I listen? Nope. I returned to the living room and settled on the couch with her to watch a movie.

Halfway through it, Rachel wanted her feet rubbed, so I rubbed her, caressing her feet as though they were her whole body. She continued with her little moans, as she ground her heels into my burning crotch. We sat like that until the movie was over, and I knew it was time for me to leave. I couldn't go through with it. I'm not a player and never enjoyed fucking with people, not even for hot sex. I was such a wimp.

Again I headed to the bathroom, to relieve my bladder before the long drive home, and I found her waiting near the door. She looked so cute standing there, her curly hair tumbling down her shoulders, her blue eyes looking up at me.

I gave her a small smile. "I really enjoyed myself," I said, though my head screamed, *Liar!* "But I'd better head out. Long drive."

Her eyelids slowly lowered as she pouted. "So soon?" she asked softly.

I nodded, though I didn't really want to leave. Only my roommate waited for me at home, and she had proclaimed me crazy for even wanting to drive out here. I didn't relish the idea of another lecture from her.

"We could always watch another movie." She stepped closer to me. I looked at her moist, kissable lips. I swallowed hard and shook my head. I needed to leave.

She took another step closer, her arms clasped behind her back as she looked up at me. I could smell her perfume. Something snapped in me. The little devil inside told me to kiss her, saying, *Don't pass up sex with a hot woman! Don't let the opportunity pass by. So what if she's married, so what if she is playing a game, so what if she just wants to experiment?* The voice was right. I was tired of straight women using me for their games then tossing me out. Why couldn't I do the same— have hot sex with this woman and toss *her* out? It was what I wanted, right?

While I was busy talking to myself, Rachel moved yet another step closer to me. I had to kiss her or open the door. I couldn't stand there arguing with myself any longer.

Fierce with determination, I suddenly grabbed her, pulled her close, and covered her plump lips with my own. I buried my hands in her hair, tugging as I mauled her lips. My tongue stabbed her mouth, dueling with hers before I raised my head and looked at her.

Rachel's eyes went wide and her mouth dropped open. She looked stunned, and for a second, I thought I had overstepped my bounds—but when her lips curved into a smile, I knew I had done the right thing. This was what she wanted.

Immediately, I turned her and pressed her petite body against the door, separating her legs with my knee and pressing into her crotch. The heat from her pussy fairly burned my black jeans, and I smiled wickedly before crushing her lips against my own again. She grabbed my shirt and tugged. Our tongues fucked each other's mouths as I continued to press my knee against her hot crotch. My hand found her breast and I played with a hard nipple through her cloth shirt. I pinched and pulled it as my hips rocked hers. She mewled against my mouth, her hands cupping my ass to bring me closer.

Somehow, we managed to make it to her bedroom before our clothes started flying off. When I finally got her damn bra off, I stared at her tits. They were perfectly round and perky. Normally, I wasn't much of a breast woman; I've had everything from fried eggs to smothering melons, so I wasn't particularly concerned about size, roundness, or girth. Still, Rachel's breasts were incredible to behold. I thought she might have had them "done," so I set out to check.

I lowered my head, trailing my tongue along one breast while my hand tweaked its nipple ring. I had never even seen fake tits, let alone felt them, so I nosed my way under the heaviness to locate the elusive giveaway scar, but I couldn't find one. My hand explored her other tit—no scar there either. They were real. Awed, I paid homage to them, sucking her hard nipple while my tongue played with the ring. Rachel wiggled and sighed, arching and tugging my hair as she gasped above my head.

Soon her hands began a quest of their own and my shirt landed on the floor, joining hers. She was greedy! Her hands were everywhere, pinching and squeezing wherever she could, scratching my back whenever I hit a spot she liked. She made the same noises she had made during dinner, but a little louder and longer. Her moans didn't stop as I lavished her stomach and tits with kisses while my fingers found the zipper of her slacks. When I pushed them down and buried my hand in her crotch, I got another surprise. Rachel had a bald pussy. Never in my life had I been with a woman who shaved completely, but Rachel did. Eager and curious, I shifted and pulled her pants completely off, tossing them aside to view her bare womanhood.

I could see the moisture glistening there, wetting a ring embedded in the hood of her clit. That ring separated her lips slightly, and I could see everything without parting them. Her cute little Tweety Bird tattoo sported a cowboy hat and boots and was nestled between her hip and pubic area, which only added to her appeal. Completely taken with the sight, I placed a soft kiss right on the hood of her clit. Her moan and slight arch told me I had the right idea, and I flicked my tongue to taste her, uttering a soft groan when her sweetness hit my taste buds.

Lying flat between her legs, I slid my hands under her ass and lifted her up, burying my face in the moisture. Her bald pussy was delightful. I didn't have to pause to pull hairs from my teeth, or choke on pubes traveling down my throat. I tasted only her sweetness and skin. Her hands fluttered, mashing my face against her pussy then grasping the bedclothes, while her hips alternated between fierce bucking and utter stillness. The more I wiggled my tongue on Rachel's exposed clit, or teased her hole with the tip of my tongue, the more erratic her movements became.

She scratched my shoulders and neck with abandon when I slipped two fingers inside her, my tongue still tormenting her clit. When I raised my head, I was happy to note that the stickiness on my face was not accompanied by the usual fur burns. Eating her was a treat. I scooted back up, and began to pump my fingers in and out—slowly at first, increasing pressure and speed until my arm was a piston and her hips were the pump. I sucked and bit her nipples, and her moans grew louder until her body stiffened, then exploded. She screamed, dragging those short nails into my back and clinging to me, while her body rode out the ride. Shaking, quivering, and shuddering, she finally collapsed on the bed.

I softly kissed Rachel, then fell beside her, a huge smile on my face. As I congratulated myself on a job well done, she suddenly was on top of me. Talk about a quick recovery! Before I said anything, she had my pants off. I was as naked as she was. It was her turn to torment—and torment she did.

She mauled my tits until my nipples swelled, then moved

down my belly, scraping my sides with her nails. My breath caught in my throat. Rachel looked fierce, determined; she licked and teased my hip bones, eliciting sounds from me that I'd never heard before. She had no hesitation, no giggles, no "is this right?" None of the nonsense I've heard in the past. This woman knew what to do to a woman. Rachel started eating my pussy, and within a few seconds she figured out what I needed. No stranger to eating pussy here! That little tongue of hers knew every magic spot inside me. She instinctively knew how hard and fast to lick me, when to insert her fingers, and how fast to pump. She fucked me with her face, her fingers, and her fist. She licked me from stem to stern, toyed with my ass, and shook my world. Within minutes, she had me over the edge, crying out her name. I lay panting, and she was smiling, goddamn it! She looked so smug and righteous, I knew I was in trouble. After all, she had told me she loved to eat.

We fucked all night, and when I finally headed home later the next day, my back burned pleasantly with the many scratches left by her nails. I had gotten fucked *and* fucked over. I had gone over to Rachel's house to teach her a lesson, but I was the one who learned a thing or two. Rachel may have been married, but she had told the truth when we met: She was into women, *deeply* into women. In fact, three years later, Rachel and I still are together, her husband gone and more scratches added to both our backs. I may have thought myself crazy when I first went over there, but now I'm the happiest dyke around.

the end

●

rachel kramer bussel

It doesn't help that she looks more beautiful now than ever. Her naturally toned face glows with the sweetest smile I will ever see, her blue eyes shining with want and need and love and pain. I want to feel like we are our own entity, existing in a private universe that no one else can pierce. Life is all about looking at her, experiencing her. She is the perfect combination of girl and woman, and she fills me with a need to hold and protect her, which leaves me raw and open—more vulnerable than any person should be.

I know all the right moves, the ways to touch her, the strokes that will make her melt and move and clutch me like she will need me forever. I know how she wants it. I need to feel like I'm the only one who can give it to her. I live for those times when the depth of her look matches the depth of my hand inside her.

As she lies there, so small and seemingly fragile, I forget her strong, stubborn core, for her doll's body looks as though it might break if I handle it improperly. Spread out in front of me, she is truly the girl of the dreams I never knew I had. I slide my fingers inside her, pushing deep into her core, knowing just where to curve and bend to get to where I want to be. I've never known another woman's body like this, navigating her pussy as easily as I trace my fingers over her face, reading her like a well-worn page of a beloved book: instantly, easily.

At this moment, seeing her hair messy and tangled like an overworked Barbie's, I want to grab it, living up to the situation's violent promise. I almost pull away, because I am not that kind of girl. I'm still getting used to wanting to hurt her, to feeling uniquely awed when I hear the sound of my hand slamming against her ass, to sometimes wanting to slap her across the face. A strange thrill rose in my throat when she cried out while I spanked her the other day.

I see the collar next to the bed, glittering brightly. It'd meant everything when I'd fastened it around her neck those countless weeks ago, transforming the airport bathroom into a private sexual sanctuary. Now, it is too bright, accusatory. Like the sweetest of forbidden fruit, her neck beckons, white and exposed, pulsing with veins and life and want. Now, when I see her neck, tender and ever needy, I can barely go near it. The pleasure would be too great. It would be a little too easy to press too hard, to enjoy hurting her for all the wrong reasons, even though I can feel her angling toward it, begging me to obliterate her for a few blessed seconds. I know what this pressure does to her, but I don't want to know. That's never been the kind of power I've wanted, even though she'd gladly give it to me, give me almost anything except what I need the most.

I want to slide back to that simple starting point, our bodies blank canvases on which to draw magnificent works of art. Maybe there is still some power left in this bed, something that flows from one of us to the other: something that binds us together. All the ways I thought I knew her have vanished, lost in a mystery too complex to solve. Too many silences and unspoken thoughts war for space between us. She is just as much a stranger to me as she was on our first date, perhaps even more so now, her mind locked away in a box for someone else's keys. Knowing only her body leaves me emptier than I would have felt if we'd never even met. Her flesh becomes a hollow victory, a prize I'm forced to return, undeserving and unwanted.

My fingers grant me nothing except access to a disembodied cunt, fitting that old-school feminist definition of pornography, a random body part with no context or meaning. I wish I could erase my sensory memory of how it feels to simultaneously fuck her, love her, and know her all at the same time. I am back to square one, vainly hoping and praying that I can make her happy.

Only this time, we have so much more to do than just fuck. We must do more than slide and scream and bite and whisper, twist and bend and push and probe. The stakes are so much higher that no orgasm will ever be enough, but I try anyway.

No matter how far I reach inside, I cannot crack her. Those eyes are a one-way mirror, reflecting the surface of something I can't see and probably don't want to see. I want to tell her I love her; I want to show her everything inside me, but when I open my mouth, I close it again just as quickly. I feel her body shaking, the tears and pain rising up like an earthquake's tremors, and I shove harder, grab her neck and push her down, anything to quell the rising tide. This may look the same as all those other times we fucked on this bed, my fingers arching and stroking, her eyes shut or staring needily at me, grabbing me when I touch her in the spot that is almost—but not quite—too much. But this is nothing like those other times, nothing like anything I've ever done before. It is like touching something totally alien, someone I never knew, someone not even human. I feel lost as I touch her, my heart so far away I hardly know how to act. I can see that I am not bridging the gap, but I can't stop myself. I try to pretend that her moans, her wetness—these external signals of desire—actually mean she is mine. But there is no way to make her come. I cannot erase the other girl's touch. I am not yet thinking about her and the other girl, wondering how she touches her: I don't want to know, yet I need to—I need to see them together like I need to see a car accident's wreckage as I speed by. But that will all come in time, in those freestanding hours of numbed shocks, those lost weekends when she invades my head and will not leave.

She has written me a letter, as requested, giving me exact blueprints for how to fuck her: how to take her up against the wall, how to tie her up, tease her, taunt her, and hold out even when she protests. I want nothing more than to be able to follow these instructions, which, by now, I don't even need, because I know how to trigger her. I can get her to go from laughing to spreading her legs in the briefest of moments. I know exactly how to touch her, where to stroke and bite and slap to give both of us what we need, but that is no longer enough. I don't have it in me to be the kind of top she wants, one who can blank out everything except that viciously visceral urge to pummel, pound, and punish. That urge is too clearly real, too close to the unspoken pain, the words that will come later. When I hit her, I know what it means. There can be no erotic power exchange when she holds all the real power. I have enough soul left in me to know that sex should not be a mechanical obligation.

I reach, reach, reach inside her, desperately searching, hoping to wrench us back to wherever we are supposed to be, back to where we were—a week, a month, a lifetime ago. I draw out this process, watching myself from afar as my hand slides inside her, as I lube myself up and try to cram all of me into her, trying to make a lasting impression. I have my entire hand inside her, yet I feel more removed from her than ever. She might as well still be in Florida. She might as well still be a stranger. This might as well be our first date, when I laughed so much because I was so nervous. I wish this were any of those early nights in our relationship, even the ones where I was so drunk and afraid, so powerless and unsure; anything would be better than this slow death, this mutual withering that renders us nothing more than two girls in a room, tears in our eyes as an ocean of questions and scars and hurt forms between us. I can't predict what will come after this most pregnant of silences, I can't know the depths of pain that will puncture me beyond the horrors of my imagination, and I can't know that I will regret everything I did wrong.

She turns over on her stomach, hiding her face from my searching eyes, and I fumble to reconnect, trying to slide into her like nothing is wrong, like it's just a matter of finding a comfortable angle. I have finally had enough. I cannot continue the charade that suggests pressing myself against her will fill all the gaps that still exist between us. But for whatever twisted reasons we need this final time. And this is the last time, because nothing is worth feeling so utterly and completely alone while you're fucking your girlfriend. No power trip or blazing orgasm, no heart-pounding breathless finish, no sadistic impulse or mistaken nostalgia is worth this much pain.

I don't know how to say what I have to. How can I ask her questions when I don't want to hear the answers? There's no book I can read that will teach me how to make her G spot tell me her secrets, those fantasies and dreams that don't come from her pussy but from her heart. The end, it turns out, is nothing like the beginning. There is no promise of something more, some grand future of possibility, the infinite ways of knowing each other just waiting to be discovered. There is no hope that we can merge into anything greater than the sum of our parts. As we end, our relationship flashes before my eyes, like a life is said to do at death. I see moments, fragments—my hand up her skirt on the street, taking her so fiercely in the doorway of a friend's apartment that she can barely sink down to the ground, her body on her knees in the bathroom, surprising me as she buries her face into me. I see myself grinding the edge of a knife along her back, slapping her tits until they are raw and red—but these moments are so far away right now, like someone else's pornographic memories. They don't make me smile, and I don't want them anymore. I want to bury myself in her and never let go; I want to hold on to something that has fluttered away in the wind, fine as the glittering sparkles in her eyes—miniscule and opaque, too minute to recapture. But all I can do is back away, as slowly as I can, so slowly that it seems I am hardly moving, and before I know it, I, and she, we, are gone.

the best-laid plans

●

delane daugherty

She slid into the restaurant booth, surrounded by a delicate cloud of vanilla spice perfume and a devastating air of confidence. Dressed in jeans and a tight T-shirt, silver hanging from her earlobes and neck, she smiled, knowing she had me then and there. I knew her eyes were brown, knew quite a bit about her from our mutual friend Jay, but I couldn't allow myself to look into those eyes. I couldn't gaze at her mouth as she talked and smiled, or at her fingers as they unconsciously caressed the neck of the bottle of beer Jay had ordered for her. I sat there in awe of her beauty, in awe of her life. She was exactly the person I had always wanted to be.

"Delane," Jay said to me at last, "this is Malory."

"Hello," I said awkwardly, feeling like a schoolgirl with an unrequited crush. Malory licked her lips and smiled again, a smile that dripped with expert sensuality, causing me to turn away, questioning my intentions.

Five years of hearing about Malory, and knowing she had been hearing about me, had not prepared me for this meeting. I couldn't imagine I was making a very good first impression; I automatically fell back on the only thing I had known for the last five years—fussing over my daughter Kelsey, who sat beside me.

We ate our food and relied heavily on Jay to keep the conversation going. "Delane's a teacher," he told Malory.

"You must love children," she said, voicing a quick assumption.

I shrugged self-consciously. "I just kind of fell into it, wanting to be with Kelsey when she was younger."

"And you moved from Los Angeles because…?" Malory lifted an inquisitive eyebrow.

"Raising a daughter alone in L.A. seemed a little overwhelming."

"That's amazing." She took a swig of beer. "Picking up and moving to a new state where you know no one is a very courageous thing to do."

"You may be overly generous with your perceptions, but thank you."

Silence surrounded the table again, until Jay offered some more information. "Malory's a business major."

I gulped my coffee and managed once again to avoid her eyes, wondering how Jay had ever talked her into this. Beautiful, intelligent, confident, and obviously going somewhere with her life—somewhere I had planned to be. What redeeming quality could she possibly find in me? A woman who ran to a small town in search of anonymity, only to find herself alone, surrounded by kids, with the amazingly magnanimous inclusion of the first edition of *Loving Someone Gay* in the public library providing the only hint of a gay community. I wondered if Jay had told her that it had been five years since I had been in a relationship. Five years since I had held and kissed a woman.

The evening ended as awkwardly as it began, with me following Malory out to the parking lot, watching every nuance of every move she made. I drank her in, wanting so much to have a piece of her life, to be what she was, to go where she was going.

I never thought I'd see her again.

***

"Malory called!" Jay exclaimed the following afternoon. "She wants to come over for a Jacuzzi tonight."

"You're kidding?"

"No. She liked you." The accomplished matchmaker smiled.

"The bar scene can't be *that* dismal these days."

"Ah, come on. Why is this so hard for you to believe?"

I took a deep breath. "Look at me. I'm a mother, a teacher. I live in a hermetically sealed closet in a tiny, politically incorrect town a thousand miles away."

"Five years ago you would've been all over this opportunity."

I looked at my closest friend in the world. Had he forgotten who I had become? "You're right. Five years ago I wouldn't have given a second thought to pursuing Malory. Five years ago I was out and proud. Five years ago I didn't have a daughter to protect from hate crimes." I looked down at my shaking hands. "But as it is now, I don't remember how to flirt, how to gaze into someone's eyes without turning away. I can't even imagine the feel of a woman next to me anymore."

Jay sat next to me and put his arm around my shoulders. "What happened to Faith was horrible. There's no denying that. But that was a long time ago. And you have done an exemplary job in raising and protecting Kelsey, but to what end?"

I turned, wiping away a tear.

"How long do you plan to keep people at a distance?" he continued. "How long will you allow yourself to be lonely for the sake of fear?"

The cool night air mixed with the chlorine-scented steam

that emanated from the Jacuzzi. Malory already sat in the bubbling water, her dark hair pushed away from her face, floating
on the surface of the water around her. My stomach threat-
ened mutiny as I slid off my robe and stepped into the Jacuzzi
beside her. The heat of the water—and her presence—simultaneously burned and soothed my skin.

"Nice night," she commented, looking into the sky.

"It's beautiful," I replied, thankful for easy small talk. "It's nice
to see stars again. It's usually too cloudy in Oregon to see any."

"It must be difficult to live with continual rainfall after having grown up here."

"I love it."

Perplexed, she knitted her thick eyebrows, and I explained:
"I've always preferred gray, rainy, dismal days to annoyingly
bright and sunny ones."

She nodded and smiled slyly. "That says a lot about you."

We laughed, and in her laughter I felt peace, a peace that
had long been elusive, even forgotten. But, nonetheless, this
peace scared the hell out of me.

Jay appeared then, offering Malory a beer and me some
coffee.

"You don't drink?" Malory asked.

"Not anymore. It's not very conducive to motherhood."

"Kelsey's asleep now. Go ahead," she urged.

"No, thanks." I took the coffee from Jay. "There are some
things you just can't go back to."

"And some you can," Jay quipped as he returned to the house.

Malory and I relaxed a bit as we drank, and before long we
were exchanging coming-out stories, tales of family betrayal,
and descriptions of ex-lovers.

"So…" Malory began slowly after a long drink of beer and
settling down further into the soothing water. "Where's
Kelsey's father?"

I stared at her incredulously.

"Did I say something wrong?" she asked.

"No, I just assumed Jay had told you."

"He told me you had been raising your daughter with your girlfriend and that she…" Malory paused, as if deciding whether to say the word. "She died unexpectedly."

I exhaled. "I guess that's an innocuous way of putting it."

"I'm sorry. If you don't want to talk about it—"

"No, no. It's OK. You asked." I took a deep breath, prepared to open a door that I had attempted long ago to slam and lock. "Faith was Kelsey's mother. We both were."

"She was artificially inseminated?"

I nodded. "When Faith returned to work after her maternity leave, one of her supervisors saw a picture of the three of us on her desk. He followed her out to her car that night." I stopped suddenly.

"That's OK, you don't have to go on." She reached for my hand, which rested on the ledge of the Jacuzzi. The touch surprised me, and I stared at our fingers nestled together, so natural, so right.

"It's all right. It was a lifetime ago." I exhaled slowly. "Faith was raped and beaten. She died the next day in a hospital room her mother had succeeded in barring me from."

"Oh, my God." Malory's grip tightened. The contact was at once comforting and exhilarating.

"So here I am now, after two years of a custody battle with Faith's mother and three years of a self-imposed exile from the real world."

"That wasn't necessarily the real world. That was more than anyone should have to go through. But I think it's time you stop paying for it."

I turned to her, and looked for the first time into her golden-brown eyes.

"Your strength is real. My admiration for you is real. This…" She lifted my hand and brought it to her mouth. "This is real." She kissed the top of my hand softly, and the feeling of her lips made me cringe with excitement and wince with uneasiness.

"You don't have to be scared anymore."

I walked her to her car and leaned against the door beside her. The currents running between our still-warm bodies were apparent, intoxicating, unnerving.

"Can I see you tomorrow?" she asked.

"Yes," I whispered, having watched her mouth as it formed words that defied my logic. I turned away, uncomfortable with the sensations she caused in me, but she caught my chin with her fingers, turned my face back to hers.

"Don't turn away from this." Her eyes glowed beautifully with her conviction.

"This is very unfamiliar territory."

"That's the best kind." Her hand moved to the back of my neck and pulled me closer to her. Our lips met tentatively, but my defenses, my uncertainty, were soon swept away and replaced by nothing but the feel of her next to me, the reality of her mouth, breath, tongue, and hands on me.

"Good night," she said after I'd lost myself in a short eternity of her kisses. "See you tomorrow."

I watched her get into her car and drive away, back lights glowing in the distance, and I stood in the middle of the street, left to wonder how the touch of a stranger could feel like coming home.

The next night, I breathed deeply of the night air that blew through the car's open window, trying to calm my stomach and the frenetic thoughts that ran through my mind.

Without looking at me, Malory asked, "Do you want to go out?"

"Sure. It's been quite a while since I've been in a bar."

"You know," she said after almost ten minutes of apparent concentration on L.A.'s labyrinth of a freeway system, "it's Saturday night. The bars are going to be so crowded, we won't be able to talk. Maybe we should just go to my house."

Her lack of subtlety was staggering, but I played along, despite my jagged nerves. "We don't have to stay long. I'd kind of like to see if the bars are the same after all these years."

She ran her right hand through her wavy hair and laughed. "Well, the cover's a lot more now. It would be ridiculous to pay it and then leave." She turned her head slightly and looked at me from the corners of her eyes. "You'll be safe, I promise."

I said nothing, knowing she never had any intention of going out. I wondered suddenly if she meant to take me home and seduce me out of pity. Maybe Jay had put her up to it. But, as if on cue, she touched my hand, and her touch was so genuine, so unfeigned, that it pushed that thought from my head. I took a deep breath and held on.

Malory's apartment was very eclectic, not the typical student's dwelling; it possessed a style that was undeniably her own. She gave me a tour, got me a drink, introduced me to her cats, and put on a k.d. lang CD.

We sat on the couch and started a casual conversation: jobs, future careers, goals. As I listened to her and petted the cat that had jumped onto my lap, I wondered if the anxiety that coursed through me was obvious.

She stopped short in the middle of telling me about one of her business courses. "Excuse me, Harvey," she said as she pushed the cat off my lap. She caught my eyes with her own as she pulled me to her. "I've got to kiss you again," she said deeply.

Suddenly my nervousness vanished; something in me shifted. I knew what was happening, knew it was what needed to happen. I embraced it, drank it and her in, a sip of water after a long, life-threatening drought. I kissed her with a ferocity that surprised her, and, when she drew her head back and opened her eyes, I took her hand and stood up with her. Without a word, I turned and led her down the hall to her bedroom.

"You're just full of surprises," she marveled.

"Sit down," I whispered and gently pushed her onto the bed. I took off my blazer and knelt in front of her, not taking my eyes from hers.

My fingers obliged themselves, plunging into her thick hair, dancing upon her soft neck. I brought my mouth to hers and, holding her face in my hands, I felt her need almost as strong as my own.

With my mouth still on hers, still immersed in the magic of her kiss, my hands began to undo the buttons of her shirt. Each button I opened offered me more access to her silky skin, and my fingers ached to touch the exposed flesh.

When the last button was undone, I eased the shirt over her shoulders and off her arms. She broke our kiss and looked at me, wide-eyed. "This is not how I had planned this seduction scene."

I smiled, softly licking at her lips. "You know what they say about the best-laid plans."

She smiled reluctantly, looking down at my mouth. "But…"

"Shh." I put a finger to her lips and she kissed it, opening her mouth to it, encircling it with her tongue. Captivated, I watched her, seeing fire in her eyes. She silently demanded to be sated.

I let my eyes slowly take in the rest of her. She wore a dark green satin bra, which accentuated her creamy white skin. Deprived for so long, my senses swirled around me as I put my mouth and tongue on her warm skin at last. I kissed her neck and collarbone, inhaling her sweet aroma, hearing the subtle changes in her breathing. My hands inched their way around her back and unfastened her bra.

The satin slid off easily, and there was no longer anything between her perfect breasts and my hungry eyes, hands, mouth. She moaned when I caressed them, my fingers working their way to her nipples, but instead of my fingers, she felt my mouth and she inhaled sharply.

I breathed warm breath on her nipple, then teased it with my tongue, licking circles around it before finally taking it into my mouth and sucking on it. Her moans intensified, and as I immersed myself in the pleasures of holding, touching, licking, and sucking each breast, I soon learned the exact pressure she preferred, the pressure that caused her hips to move in a way that I could no longer ignore.

I kissed my way back to her mouth, which was open and warm, and delved into her luscious kiss once again. Without breaking our kiss, I pulled her up and began unzipping her pants. Giving me no protest this time, she stepped out of her pants as they fell to the floor.

I took a step back and gazed at her, watched my fingers as they glided over the gentle curves of her hips and thighs. Her beauty was palpable.

She sat on the bed again, watching me watch her, then she lay back, throwing her arms over her head. k.d. lang sang "Wash Me Clean" as I removed my tank top and bra, then slid my own pants off. Malory reached for me as I stood over her, and I allowed her to pull me on top of her, thrilling to the buttery sensation of her skin against mine.

We kissed, and her feather-soft hands moved across my shoulders, down my back. She took hold of my hips and moved against them, creating a gentle rhythm between us. Her leg slid between mine, and her grip on my hips tightened as she guided my body up and down against her thigh. As she started to turn, started to lay her body on mine, I resisted and instead pulled her up to a sitting position.

"Delane, I want to please you," she pouted.

I shook my head, lowered myself between her legs. "I want to taste you."

With trembling hands I touched her knees, brought them in close to my body, enclosing me within her. My fingers crept up her thighs, and, watching the reactions that embellished her face, I became mesmerized. She closed her eyes and parted her lips slightly as I brought my mouth to her legs. Holding her hips still with my hands, I kissed and licked up each thigh, taking my time, savoring every inch of her.

My hands moved up to her breasts as my tongue gently, slowly, barely lapped at her wet satin underwear. She grasped my hands and pressed them harder against her breasts and tilted her hips toward my mouth. I withdrew and watched her arch her back in vain, straining to feel my mouth on her. I watched my hands beneath hers, working together, kneading her breasts, and I felt my own desire, torrential and urgent, feeding off hers.

My mouth returned to her, licking slowly, lightly, despite her need, tasting her through the fabric. She rocked her hips, moved her wetness against my face, then leaned back, bracing herself with her hands. I took my hands from her breasts, and as if finally opening a long-awaited gift, I carefully moved her underwear aside, seeing her in all of her beautiful splendor, wet, expectant, wanting me.

With my tongue finally against her velvety flesh, she moaned and held my head to her, writhed against my mouth as I licked her delicately, gently sucking her clitoris. Her moans gradually turned into words, urgings that intoxicated me, and I closed my eyes, surrendered myself to the feel, the smell, the taste of her.

Her legs surrounding me, her hands pushing me further into her, my mouth maintained its lingering pace, creating a steady motion that melded with the rocking of her hips.

Sensing her orgasm building, I moved my mouth, and she thrust against me as my tongue entered her. Her breathing overpowered k.d.'s crooning and filled the room as my tongue slid in and out of her in a rhythm that brought her to the peak of her release but did not allow her over the top.

I opened my eyes to see that she was watching me. She removed her hand from my hair and put it where mine was, holding her underwear out of my mouth's way. "Touch yourself," she instructed.

I obeyed, removing my hand and slipping it into my underwear, feeling my own wetness as my tongue remained surrounded by hers.

Seeing that I had heeded her command, she closed her eyes again and lay back. I licked her fingers, sucked them as they rested in her juices. She arched against me, trying to get me back inside her, but my tongue teased her, tempted her, did not quite enter her, swirling, flicking, sucking, gradually building her back to the place where she could take no more, would ache for release.

My fingers' movements on me matched my tongue's movements on her, and I pressed against my hand as her body pressed against my face. When her breath was ragged, seething with the desire I had created, having been to the edge and back too many times to count, I dipped my finger inside her, entering her slightly then retreating, over and over again, a little further each time, until her hips lifted forcefully with each penetration, engulfing the length of my finger, then two.

I continued licking her as my fingers thrust into each of us, their pace quickening with every tilt of her hips. I could no longer distinguish her wetness from my own, or tell which of my hands was in whom. Eyes closed, we had merged into one, feeling the same spark, succumbing to the same flame, reaching for the same culminating combustion.

Her body shuddered against my face and hand, and we came

together as her voice filled the room. Fingers of both hands stilled to the spasms that clenched them.

She eased herself over the edge of the bed and sat in front of me, allowing my fingers to remain inside of her, part of her now. She said nothing, but she kissed me, held me, caressed my soul.

"Are you OK?" Malory asked as she drove me back to Jay's house, to the staid existence I had thought was my reality.

I smiled, held onto her hand in my lap. "I'm great."

"Surprised?" she asked, raising one of her seductive eyebrows.

I tilted my head questioningly.

"At my submission…"

"No. More at my assertion. I didn't think I was still capable of that."

"Nothing's ever lost forever." She glanced at me quickly, then pulled the car over to the side of the road. She turned to me. "The way you look right now…the easy smile, the unabashed eye contact, the self-confidence… That wasn't there three days ago. I want you to hold on to that. I want to see that in you the next time we meet."

She reached for me, and we embraced, soft arms encircling my body once again. I drew strength from them. I drew resolution from them.

"Be happy," she whispered in my ear. "And stay happy."

"I plan on it."